The temptation to kiss her overwhelmed him, and he lowered his mouth and brushed her lips with his.

She felt so dainty in his arms, so tender, and his own hunger rippled through him.

But her startled gasp made him pull back, and he cursed himself.

He was a selfish bastard. The kiss hadn't been for her, but for him. Hearing the despair in her voice had done something to him, stirring up feelings he didn't want to feel, especially for her.

"I'm sorry," he said in a low voice as he backed toward the door. He couldn't shake the unsettling feeling that he had frightened her with his kiss.

Need, hunger, the desire to soothe her—to make love to her—churned through him. Needs he couldn't pursue.

RITA HERRON

SILENT NIGHT SANCTUARY

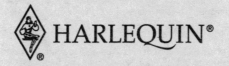

TORONTO • NEW YORK • LONDON
AMSTERDAM • PARIS • SYDNEY • HAMBURG
STOCKHOLM • ATHENS • TOKYO • MILAN • MADRID
PRAGUE • WARSAW • BUDAPEST • AUCKLAND

To Allison & Denise, two great editors
with fabulous advice!

Recycling programs
for this product may
not exist in your area.

ISBN-13: 978-0-373-69364-1
ISBN-10:   0-373-69364-8

SILENT NIGHT SANCTUARY

www.eHarlequin.com

Printed in U.S.A.

ABOUT THE AUTHOR

Award-winning author Rita Herron wrote her first book when she was twelve, but didn't think real people grew up to be writers. Now she writes so she doesn't have to get a *real* job. A former kindergarten teacher and workshop leader, she traded her storytelling for kids for romance, and writes romantic comedies and romantic suspense. She lives in Georgia with her own romance hero and three kids. She loves to hear from readers so please write her at P.O. Box 921225, Norcross, GA 30092-1225, or visit her Web site at www.ritaherron.com.

Books by Rita Herron

CAST OF CHARACTERS

Leah Holden—A woman desperate to find her missing sister and protect the past....

Gage McDermont—A detective determined to solve the case, even if he has to expose Leah's secrets.

Ruby Holden—An innocent seven-year-old caught in a web of lies.

Carmel Foster—She lost her child. Has she taken Ruby as a replacement?

Amos Trevett—He has a record as a child predator but claims he's innocent. Is he lying?

Jerry McDermont—Gage's adopted brother resented Gage. Did he hurt Leah as revenge?

Dr. Donnie Burkham—He was furious at Leah for implying he abused his son. Has he done something to Ruby to get back at Leah?

Warren Cox—A mentally challenged young man who befriends little girls. Did he kidnap Ruby?

Charlie Driscill—The deputy will do anything to enforce the bond of silence the teenagers entered into, and to keep the past forgotten.

Harry Wiggins—He was Leah's friend. But did he protect her when he should have?

Jameson Mansfield—The town lawyer who wants to keep the past quiet—how far would he go to keep the others from talking?

Evan Rutherford—The high school football coach was a football legend in high school. Did he hurt Leah and cover it up?

Chapter One

The wind whipping through the paper-thin walls of Leah Holden's North Carolina mountain cabin whistled, shrill and violent, jarring her from a deep sleep. Or had the sound been a scream?

A child's scream...

Ruby?

Leah vaulted from her bed and raced to her seven-year-old sister's room, praying she'd been wrong. Through the half-open door, Christmas lights from the tiny tree inside sparkled red and gold and silver.

But when she rushed inside, Ruby's bed was empty.

"Ruby!" Her heart pounded as she scanned the interior, the dark shadows, the rumpled bedding, the closet where her sister had made a playhouse for her dolls.

No Ruby.

The curtains flapped wildly, the chill in the room sending icy fear through her.

The window was open. It had been shut when Leah had gone to bed.

Frantic, she flipped on the overhead light, her gaze landing on the teddy bear that had been slashed to pieces on Ruby's bed. A note lay in the midst of the cotton stuffing, and nausea lurched in her stomach.

CALL THE POLICE AND THE CHILD DIES.

She screamed in terror, panic clenching her chest as a dozen horrific scenarios assaulted her. Ruby, kidnapped. Being tortured. Abused. Molested. Murdered.

The room swirled in a blinding sea of white and she gripped the edge of the brass bed, struggling not to pass out. This couldn't be happening.

Sanctuary was supposed to be a safe little town. A haven for families—a close-knit community.

But a cold emptiness filled Ruby's room. The sight of her Pippi Longstocking doll brought tears to Leah's eyes. Ruby loved her Pippi doll just as Leah had loved the colorful character when she was a child. After her mother had died, Leah had moved back home to take care of Ruby, and they'd started reading the Pippi books together.

Leah's hand trembled as she ran to the den for the phone. The message on the note echoed in her head and she hesitated. Every horrific TV-show scenario flashed through her mind.

Maybe she shouldn't call the police.

But time was important. And how could she handle this alone?

She needed the police to issue an AMBER Alert, start searching, set up road blocks, put Ruby's picture on the news, call the FBI… She needed them to find Ruby.

Terrified, she punched in the number. Ruby was all the family she had left. She had to find her.

THE IMAGE OF THE dead boy's face would haunt Detective Gage McDermont for the rest of his life.

Thirteen years old and he'd been murdered on the sidewalk by a man who should have still been in jail.

All because the kid had tried to do what was right: testify against a lowlife scumbag for beating his mother to a bloody pulp.

In the end, she had died. And Rodney Kemple had walked on a damn technicality and shot the kid in the chest.

Guilt pressed against Gage's lungs, making it impossible to breathe. He had promised Tommy Beringer that he'd protect him.

And he had failed.

So had the system Gage had sworn to uphold.

He balled his hands into fists as he waited in the chief's office, wanting to pound something again, just like he'd pounded Kemple's face when he'd finally caught up with him. He'd have finished the guy off if his partner hadn't interceded and dragged him away.

The chief walked in, his granitelike face showing a mixture of anger and disdain. Gage had worked for the

Raleigh Police Department for eight years, and he and Drew Hardy had almost come to blows before, but the past year things had grown even more strained. The chief seemed to be more interested in politics than catching perps, and Gage had told him so more than once.

Hadn't gone over well with the chief.

"What in the hell were you thinking, McDermont?" A vein bulged in Hardy's wide throat. "You nearly beat Kemple to death."

"He deserved far worse than he got, and you know it, Chief." Gage pushed to his feet, anger rolling off him. "He put a bullet in that kid's chest."

"You had him under arrest," the chief barked. "Now we have police brutality charges to deal with and IA on our butts. Are you trying to make this department look bad?"

"You're worried about the damn department?" Fury turned Gage's voice to ice. "What about that poor kid? The one we promised to protect?" He struggled with the hate churning in his gut. "What about justice? When did our jobs stop being about that?"

The chief leveled him with a lethal stare. "I'm trying to see that justice is done," he growled. "Within the law. And your actions may just enable this guy to walk."

"He won't walk," Gage snapped. "We've got the gun with his prints on it, and Beringer's shirt."

Chief Hardy slammed his hand on the desk. "You've been walking the line for months, McDermont. But this time you went too far."

Gage crossed his arms. "If you want an apology from me, you're wasting your time."

The chief's furious stare met his. "In that case, I'm ordering you to take a voluntary leave of absence. Take some time off, get your head back on straight," he hissed. "Hell, if you need to see a counselor, the department can set you up."

"And if I don't?"

His voice dropped and he leaned forward. "Then I'll be forced to suspend you."

Rage, frustration and disbelief rallied inside Gage like a storm ready to unfold.

His job was his life.

But he was fed up with gangs, street thugs and having to adhere to the bureaucratic BS that protected criminals' rights and left the victims vulnerable and without justice.

And if he had it to do over again, he'd beat Kemple even worse.

"What's it going to be, McDermont?"

Gage removed his badge from inside his leather jacket, ripped off his shoulder holster, put them both on the desk and then walked out.

All he'd ever wanted to do was be a cop.

But there were other ways to get justice. Maybe it was time he went out on his own.

RUBY HAD BEEN missing for seven days now.

Seven days of pure torture.

Tears blurred Leah's eyes as she stared at the gifts stacked beneath the glittering tree. Christmas was three days away.

Ruby had to be home by then. The house was so empty, the silence deafening.

When she got back, they'd make sugar cookies and hot chocolate, and Ruby would squeal with delight when she discovered the games and craft sets under the tree.

And Santa was supposed to bring a kitten. Not that Ruby completely believed in Santa, but she still pretended.

Leah's breath caught. Today the locals had called off the search teams that had combed the woods. Had essentially given Ruby up for dead.

Leah paced to the window and studied the empty backyard swing dangling in the wind. Ruby loved that swing.

But she might never sit in it again. Might never run across the yard or skip rope or climb the ancient oak to the tree house they had built together last summer.

Thunder rumbled across the gray sky, her mood as dark as the threatening storm. It was too cold for a child to survive out in those woods. Too dangerous.

Coyotes roamed the mountains, along with bears and mountain lions. And there were tales of mountain men who lived in the wild—who'd never been civilized. Strange things had happened along the Appalachian trail and in the deep recesses of the forests. People had gone missing and never been found.

Stories of cults and gypsy clans who performed strange rituals circulated. There were also rumors of ghosts haunting the area, the agonized souls of people who were killed in the battles between Native Americans and those who'd driven them from their homes during the Trail of Tears.

What if one of the animals had gotten Ruby? Or one of the mountain men? What would he do to her?

What had he already done?

Was Ruby lost somewhere, terrified and alone? Hurting or locked up in some scary place?

Was she…

No, Leah wouldn't give up hope. She couldn't.

But the local police hadn't been able to find her. Not that she trusted them, especially with Charlie Driscill, a guy from her old high school, as the deputy and acting sheriff. He was following in his father's footsteps, preparing to take over as sheriff when his dad retired soon.

She'd considered the fact that her own secrets might have played a part in Ruby's kidnapping, that the kidnapper was someone from her past—someone from that terrible night eight years ago—but everyone in town had been questioned and supposedly had alibis.

She'd even wondered if Ruby's father had taken her. But that was impossible. Ruby's father didn't even know she existed.

Had she made a mistake in calling the police? Would the kidnapper have contacted her if she hadn't?

A sob choked her. She'd been second-guessing herself for days now, praying for a phone call or a message that someone had seen her sister. But that phone call had never come.

GAGE STARED AT THE NEWS broadcast of the update on Ruby Holden's kidnapping, emotions rising to the surface. He still couldn't believe there had been a kidnapping in his hometown. Not in Sanctuary.

The news clip summarized the past few days of the search and then showed the deputy sheriff, Charlie Driscill, approaching Leah Holden. He'd said, "I'm sorry, but we're calling off the search team." Then Leah collapsed in a fit of tears.

Seven days missing—he understood the reasoning behind calling off the search. By now, the kidnapper would have left the area.

Or the child was dead.

Every hour a child was missing lessened the chances that she would be found alive.

He watched as neighbors surrounded Leah, supporting her, and frowned.

There had been no ransom call. No word. No physical evidence except that shredded teddy bear and the note warning Leah not to call the police.

So what was the kidnapper's motive? Was he a pedophile? Someone who'd lost a child and wanted to replace it with another? A crazy lunatic who simply saw an opportunity?

He glanced at the screen again. Leah looked so lost, so devastated….

He had to do something.

Not that he wanted to see her again after all these years, but she needed help. And a child was in danger.

The past week he'd decided to start his own private investigative firm specializing in children's cases. In memory of Ramona Samples, the woman who'd helped him find a home with the McDermonts, he'd decided to call his agency Guardian Angel Investigations. He planned to hire other detectives to work for him, ex-cops or military men, as well as security and computer specialists. GAI would step in when the police or feds failed.

Or when a client chose not to call the police.

And he'd jump-start his agency by finding Leah's sister.

Leah had called in the locals, but after seeing her plea on the news, he sensed she was hiding something. If she'd done something to her sister, he'd nail her ass to the wall.

But memories of Leah in high school returned and he couldn't believe she'd hurt anyone. He'd harbored a crush on her in high school and had planned to meet her at a party once, but then she'd hooked up with his brother.

He'd never spoken to her after that day. And it had caused a rift between him and Jerry.

Maybe moving back home for a while would enable him to mend fences with Jerry. After all, Jerry had probably changed. He owned a construction company and had built neighborhoods all around Sanctuary.

Gage turned off the TV, tucked the newspaper photo of Ruby inside his bomber jacket, climbed in his Explorer and headed toward Sanctuary.

He'd find out what happened to this little girl and make the person who'd abducted her pay.

HE WATCHED Leah Holden's house from the top of the ridge with his telephoto lens, the frigid December air biting at his neck and hands. His skin was raw, dry and chafed, but he barely noticed. Rage heated his bloodstream, making it flow thick and hot through his system.

Leah shouldn't have called the police. He'd never expected her to, counting on her fear and cowardice to keep her quiet.

The bitch should have heeded the warning. If she had, she'd have the kid back by now, and life could go on as normal.

But no, she'd called the damn cops.

She'd be sorry she ever came back to town. Ever messed with their lives. Ever lived.

Because of her, Ruby might have to die.

Chapter Two

Shoulders tight with tension, Gage left the beltway for the curvy roads to the Blue Ridge Mountains. He'd thought he'd never return to Sanctuary—but the moment he'd seen Leah Holden in trouble, he knew he had no choice.

The roads grew more narrow and winding as the hills and ridges encroached. Thick, tall pines and evergreens covered the sloping hills, the deep recesses, the cliffs—perfect hiding places for moonshiners, meth labs, domestic violence and possible criminals. Fishers, hikers, campers and vacationers as well as locals came and went. Anyone could have been a possible suspect in a child abduction.

He wound through the heart of Sanctuary, past the town square with the park, and the local storefronts decorated for the holidays with bows, lights and wreaths. He recognized Delilah's Diner, the drugstore which still boasted an old-fashioned soda fountain, and of course Magnolia Manor, where he'd lived for a while.

Remembering how it felt to be a lost, lonely little kid, he wondered how Ruby was holding up.

And if she was still alive.

Leaving the small downtown area, he drove past signs pointing to several rental cabins and the creek gurgling along the ridges, then turned into the entrance to the small rural development where Leah's family had lived. It was an older subdivision which, judging from the yards filled with toys and bikes, was still home to many families.

He'd read the reports—Leah had a degree in education, and had been teaching at Sanctuary Elementary. She made a modest teacher's salary but had no money to speak of.

Could explain why there had been no ransom request. The kidnapper hadn't wanted money. He'd wanted Ruby.

Not a place he wanted to go…but he had to.

In spite of the fact that winter had descended, pansies bloomed around Leah's mailbox, and a bird feeder was perched in the front yard, making the place look homey and well kept.

Holiday lights dangled from the roof with a Santa and sleigh next to the chimney, and a Christmas tree glowed through the front window.

A bicycle with a purple basket leaned against the open carport—the lack of a garage was a reminder that the home had been built forty years earlier. Hot-pink roller skates had been left in front of the bike as if the little girl had kicked them off before running inside. He parked in the drive, noticed Leah drove a small minivan, and frowned. Everything here reeked of family—a loving family.

One he'd never had. One a kid deserved.

Bracing himself to see Leah again, he strode up to the front porch and rang the bell.

A minute later, a fragile voice came from the other side of the door. "Who is it?"

"Gage McDermont, Leah. I'm here about your sister."

The sound of locks being turned echoed from inside, and she opened the door, her eyes wide.

"Gage McDermont?" she gaped at him, obviously surprised to find him on her doorstep. "Do you know something about Ruby?"

The sight of her red-rimmed, swollen eyes and her trembling, petite frame made his stomach knot. She'd been pretty as a young girl, but she'd matured and her beauty sucker punched him.

He forced himself to refrain from pulling her into his arms to comfort her.

He'd find out what happened to her sister. But he wouldn't get involved with Leah personally. She'd broken his heart once.

He wouldn't let her do it again.

LEAH CLUTCHED THE TISSUE in her hands and tried to control her trembling as she stared at the man on her porch.

A man she'd thought she was in love with at age sixteen.

A man who'd ditched her the night she'd gone to a party to see him.

The last man she wanted to see—or accept help from—now.

"I thought you were on the Raleigh police force," she said, her voice shaking.

"I was." The wind tossed his dark, curly hair across his forehead, his brown eyes so intense that something flamed low in her belly, reminding her that he'd always caused a heated reaction within her. No other man ever had.

But she wouldn't go there again.

"I'm starting my own private detective agency." He pointed to the foyer. "Mind if I come in?"

She swayed, dizzy with fatigue and the sudden jolt of his masculine scent invading her house. He'd been tall in high school, but now he easily cleared six feet. His shoulders had broadened and his face had filled out, dark with a five-o'clock shadow.

"Leah, I really am here to help."

She clutched her bathrobe around her and stepped aside, gesturing for him to enter. Although she couldn't for the life of her figure out why he'd offered to help her. They hadn't spoken in years. "I'll make some coffee."

"Thanks. I could use some."

Needing to escape and compose herself, she rushed to the kitchen but he followed her, his gaze tracking her as she measured coffee into the filter and filled the pot with water. "There's food, too," she said inanely. "Everyone in town has brought casseroles by, but I haven't been hungry."

"No, thanks. Coffee's fine."

She nodded. "I didn't know you were back in town," she said as she reached for two mugs. Did his brother know he was back?

"I just drove in."

His husky voice sounded even deeper with age—sexier, if possible. And more dangerous.

He would ask questions just as the police had. Questions she didn't want to answer. Questions she'd avoided for years.

But the past had nothing to do with Ruby's kidnapping so why should she open up that wound?

Answering those questions would mean breaking the bond of silence she'd entered into almost a decade ago. A bond she'd agreed to against her will, but one she had accepted in order to protect her family, herself and Ruby.

She filled their mugs and offered him cream and sugar, but he took his black. Warming her hands with the cup, she led him into the den. The Christmas tree lights twinkled, the unopened gifts reminding her how empty the house was without Ruby, how desolate Christmas would be if her sister didn't come home.

Wind ripped harshly through the eaves of the old house, rattling windowpanes and shutters, adding to her chill. She motioned for him to sit down.

"I read about Ruby's disappearance," Gage said. "And I wanted to offer my services."

"I don't have much money," Leah said, lowering her gaze to stare into her mug. "You know Dad died when I was sixteen. He worked as a landscape artist but had no savings to speak of. And Mom was a receptionist at a local insurance company. What little insurance money there was had to go to Mom's hospital bills."

"I was sorry to hear about her death," Gage said, although he hadn't known Leah's family very well. "Don't worry about the money. Solving your case and finding your sister will be good publicity for my firm."

Anger seeped through her. "This is not about publicity," she said. "It's about finding Ruby, Gage."

His jaw tightened, those dark fathomless eyes raking over her. "I didn't mean it like that. I just meant that money is not an issue here. Finding your sister will be my priority."

She searched his face. "Why should you care? You haven't lived in Sanctuary for years."

He took a sip of coffee. "I had my reasons for staying away."

She glanced up and saw the strain on his face. She knew he and his brother had had issues and that he hadn't had a happy home life. The McDermont family had taken him in and Jerry had resented him.

But all the girls in high school had been in love with Gage. He was brooding, the kind of bad boy that every girl wanted. The kind who stood up for the kids who were bullied because he had no fear for himself.

"I still don't understand why you came back," Leah said.

He leaned forward and propped his elbows on his knees, studying her. "Did you read about the thirteen-year-old boy who got killed last week in Raleigh?"

She nodded.

"That was my case." His voice dropped an octave. "He died on my watch, and I lashed out at the guy who did it. He deserved it but the chief suggested I take some time off."

She sighed, tucking a strand of hair behind her ear. "I'm sorry. That poor boy."

He gave a clipped nod. "That's why I decided to start my own agency, Guardian Angel Investigations. I get to play by my own rules. If you let me, I'll do everything I can to find your sister. And I'll see that whoever kidnapped her pays."

She bit her lip, so tempted. She needed help.

But Gage? Why him?

"Is there some reason you don't want me investigating, Leah?" Gage asked. "Is there something you're trying to hide?"

Leah stiffened. Why would he ask her such a thing?

"Leah?"

"Of course not," she said. "What are you implying?"

"I just want you to be honest with me. There may be something you haven't shared that might lead us to your sister."

"I told the police everything. But maybe I shouldn't have called them." She stood and crossed to the Christmas tree, toying with a reindeer Ruby had made out of clothespins. "The note warned me not to." Emotion choked her voice. "If Ruby gets hurt or…worse, it will be my fault."

RUBY HUGGED HER Matilda doll to her chest, tears trickling down her cheeks. She wanted to go home, back to her mama's house, back to Leah.

But the man with the mask said that Leah didn't want her anymore.

A sob wrenched her throat and she rolled to her side on the hard cot, coughing at the musky smell. It was dark and cold way up here in the attic. The man had brought her here and left her all alone.

There weren't any kids to play with, no toys, no swing set, no tree house or bicycles.

No Christmas tree….

Just a few crayons and paper, and she'd almost used them all up.

She looked into the doll's eyes, her chest hurting as she thought of home and how far away it seemed. Would she ever see her four-poster bed again? The unicorn spread? The pillow her mommy had made for her?

Her sister?

Would she be home for Christmas? How would Santa ever find her here?

Chapter Three

Gage scrutinized Leah, from her facial expressions and body language to the intonations of her voice, looking for a clue to indicate she was lying.

But her tears and those luminous, sad green eyes instantly tied him in knots. So did the smell of freshly baked cookies, as if she had made a batch to welcome her sister home.

He understood her terror as well as her guilt.

And even with anguish lining her features, she was the most beautiful woman he'd seen in a long time.

But he couldn't allow himself to focus on that. This was just a case and Leah meant nothing to him.

Besides, he'd detected her moment of hesitation when he'd asked her if she was hiding something.

A moment that had confirmed his fear.

Whether or not it had anything to do with Ruby's disappearance was another story.

But he suddenly wanted to unravel the secrets she had—especially why she didn't want him here.

And why she'd avoided him in high school after she'd blown him off and hooked up with his brother.

"Leah, you can't blame yourself. Most of the time it's best for families to contact the police."

"But what if this man hurts Ruby because of me?"

"It won't do any good to second-guess yourself now. Why don't you go over everything with me and we'll see if the police might have missed something?"

She blinked back tears and nodded. "All right. If you think you can help. I'll do anything to find her, Gage."

If he'd thought she had anything to do with Ruby's disappearance, he didn't think so now. Her pain was too raw.

"I'd like to review all the information about the investigation. But first, why don't you show me Ruby's room."

Again, guilt and worry strained her face, but she moved as if on autopilot to Ruby's bedroom.

"She's in my old room," Leah said, gesturing at the lavender walls and stuffed animals covering the white, four-poster canopied bed.

He noted the unicorn bedspread, the pillowcase hand-embroidered with Ruby's name. A pair of discarded sneakers lay by the closet door, a lime-green backpack beside them. A hot-pink jacket, fuzzy gloves and hat sat near a toy box overflowing with games and dolls.

Instincts honed from years on the force kicked in, and he knew he had to remain objective and push Leah. There had to be something the police had overlooked.

"Tell me exactly what happened."

She averted her gaze, walked to the window and looked out as if seeking answers. "I woke up early that morning— it was still dark. The wind was howling but I thought I heard a scream. Maybe it was Ruby…crying out for me to save her." Her hands rose to her cheeks, wiping at tears. "But I was too late. If only I'd woken up a few minutes earlier."

"Was her bed still warm when you came in?"

She turned to him, angling her head as if in thought. "I…don't remember feeling it. I panicked, then called for help. I kept thinking that if the kidnapper was trying to leave town the police could find him before he got too far away."

"There was no ransom note?"

She shook her head. "Just the note on the bed by the shredded teddy bear warning me not to call the police."

"And you haven't received any other calls or messages since?"

"No."

"Do you have any major investments, money tucked away that someone might know about?"

"No, nothing like that." She gestured at the room. "As you can see, my house is modest."

He folded his arms. "Can you think of anyone who'd want to hurt you or Ruby?"

"No, no one specific." She sighed and dragged a hand through her hair. "I've already told the police all this."

"I know, but humor me. Like I said, maybe they missed

something. Think about the school where you teach. Any parents—fathers perhaps—that you've pissed off?"

Her mouth twisted. "There was a man, a single dad, who got angry with me last month."

"What happened?"

"His son had some bruises on his chest and legs and I asked him about them, but I think the police questioned him already."

"What did the man have to say about his son's bruises?"

"That his little boy is clumsy and accident-prone."

Gage grimaced. He'd heard that before.

He moved inside the room, examining the space without touching anything. Everything indicated that a happy, normal child lived within these walls but appearances could be deceiving. "Your bedroom is on the opposite side of the house?"

"Yes. But I don't know how someone got in and took her without me hearing. It's not a big house. I mean, I thought I heard a scream, but…"

"Well, you said the wind was howling, right? Maybe it covered the noise. Or maybe she knew him." He gestured at the window. "The window lock was jimmied. That's how he got in?"

She nodded, pain darkening her eyes. "It was locked when I went to bed, but when I came in, it was open."

"And the police didn't find any DNA or fingerprints?"

"They said they didn't."

Her wording roused his suspicions "What do you mean,

they *said* they didn't? Do you have reason to believe the police might be lying?"

She jerked her head up, her eyes wide as if she'd just realized what she'd said. Oftentimes people gave the truth away innocuously.

"Leah? Is there some reason you don't trust the police or think they didn't do their jobs?"

She chewed her bottom lip before answering. "Not exactly...."

"What?"

"It's just that Charlie is the deputy now, and his father always ran everything." She shrugged. "They don't tell you much."

He'd never liked Charlie Driscill himself. Had Charlie run a shoddy investigation?

He studied the child's room, debating how much to prod Leah. A small table and chairs held a sketch pad and crayons, dolls crowded a baker's rack and books and puzzles overflowed a bookshelf. "Does your sister have a computer?"

"No, it was a sore subject between us, because she wanted her own laptop in her room, and I wouldn't allow it." Her chest rose up and down with a shaky breath. "I know how dangerous it is for kids on the Internet, so I let her use mine but only with supervision."

She had the right answers and appeared to be caring and protective. "The feds looked at my computer and found nothing," Leah added.

"Was anything else missing? Any clothes, toys?"

Her eyes darted around nervously. "Her Matilda doll is gone. She might have it with her."

So the kidnapper hadn't packed a bag to take with them. "Good. That might prove to be helpful somehow." At least in tracing her, or, if they found a body, in identifying her. But he refrained from relaying that thought.

She paced, wringing her hands together, then paused and traced her finger over a drawing Ruby had done. It was a childish sketch of a girl and a woman smiling, hands outstretched to each other in a meadow of wildflowers.

The sight of the room was obviously torturing her, so he moved toward the hall. "Let's go downstairs."

Relief softened the lines on her face. She was so petite, and fragile looking. Creamy skin, golden hair that fell in soft waves around her heart-shaped face, eyes the palest green he'd ever seen.

But the photo of the little girl burned in his pocket, reminding him to keep this strictly business. Every second counted. He didn't want another child to end up dead on his watch.

And her comment about the police bugged him. If there was some reason she didn't trust them, he needed to know what it was. It might prove to be the lead they needed to find Ruby.

LEAH STARED AT Gage's folded hands as he sat in the club chair in the den.

His hands were large, masculine, callused. A jagged

scar crisscrossed his right one, disappearing into the sleeve of his shirt.

She claimed the love seat and held Ruby's Pippi doll, gently running a finger over its long red braids. The yarn hair was coarse, not like Ruby's soft red curls.

Where was she right now? What was happening to her?

"All right, Leah. Give me a blow-by-blow of the events leading up to Ruby's abduction."

She took a deep breath. "The night before she disappeared I took Ruby to the park. They had a mini-fair with a merry-go-round and cotton candy and games."

"Did you notice anyone following or watching you and Ruby?"

She bit down on her lip and struggled to think, but she'd been caught up in Ruby's laughter and chatter, and hadn't noticed anyone. "No, I... Maybe I should have but I didn't see anything strange. There were a lot of families there—teenagers, kids laughing, running around, all excited."

"Did you lose sight of your sister at any time?"

"No, I never left her side. We played some games and rode a few rides." She paused. "I understand how important it is to watch children closely, and how quickly they can slip away."

He nodded. "Go on. What did you do then?"

"Ruby wanted a corn dog and cotton candy, and then an ice cream sundae." She remembered Ruby's shriek of joy when Leah had finally given in and allowed her the sweets. "Normally I don't let her have so much junk food, but it was our 'Fun Friday,' that's what we call it, and I caved." She shrugged helplessly, wondering if they'd ever share another Fun Friday again. Knotting her hands to compose herself, she pressed on. "Unfortunately she got an upset stomach, and went to bed as soon as we arrived home."

He narrowed his eyes and her heart pounded. "What?" she asked.

"I was just wondering if a stranger could have slipped something in her food at the fair."

A bead of perspiration trickled down the back of her neck. "I…don't know. I didn't see anyone near her food except the vendors."

He nodded but she had to wonder. If someone had followed them, was it possible? The place had been packed. They'd stopped to play dart balloons and others had squeezed beside Ruby while she'd hung back and given them space. Although she'd kept an eye on Ruby, she could have missed something.

"Leah," Gage said in a deep voice. "I understand this is difficult, but I need you to finish. Did you go to bed when Ruby did?"

She hesitated, driving her fingers through her hair. "Not right away. I locked up the house and read for a while, then turned in."

"Did you check on Ruby?"

Her gaze shot to his. "Yes, I always do. She was

sleeping peacefully, but she'd kicked off the comforter. I went in and covered her."

"And the window was closed?"

"Yes."

"Did you sleep all night?" he asked. "You didn't hear anything?"

Tears pooled in her eyes. "No, not until the morning." Her gaze lifted to his. "How could I sleep while someone was breaking in and taking her?"

"It happens, Leah." His expression softened slightly, and she decided maybe he did have a heart.

"What time did you notice she was missing?"

"I woke up right before dawn when I heard the wind screaming, and I had a bad feeling." She pressed a hand to her aching chest, drawing in a tortured breath. "I got up and ran to check on Ruby. I wanted to make sure she was tucked in, not freezing."

"And you saw the open window then?"

She nodded. "Then I saw that Ruby wasn't in her bed." Tears trickled down her cheeks, and she brushed them away. "I called her name but she didn't answer, and I panicked and flipped on the light. Then I saw the bear and the note."

And sheer terror had ripped through her.

"The police questioned the staff and vendors at the fair, didn't they?"

She nodded. "No one saw anything."

And the feds hadn't turned up anything suspicious on

them. They speculated that a vacationer or someone traveling through might have seen her, followed her home and absconded with her in the night. Obviously, whoever had kidnapped her hadn't drawn anyone's attention.

"Did you have a gardener or any workers—repairmen, cable guys, anybody like that—in before the kidnapping?"

She massaged her temple. "No. I mow my own lawn, and I don't remember any strange workers being in the neighborhood. I certainly hadn't hired any."

"I know the police already questioned the neighbors, but I'd like to do that myself." He looked at her, hard. "But first, I have to ask you, Leah. Can you think of anyone else who'd kidnap Ruby? Her father—"

"Our father died before she was born," Leah said, cutting him off. "You know that, Gage."

He stared at her for so long that she started to fidget in her seat. "I just thought that maybe your mother had met someone else.…"

"Heavens, no. My mother was always faithful to my dad."

But Leah's dad wasn't Ruby's. Had Gage somehow discovered their secret?

"How long have you been back in Sanctuary?" Gage asked.

She fisted her hands in her lap. "Since my mother died three months ago."

"Where did you live before that?"

"In a condo in Atlanta. I was teaching there, but decided to move back to my mom's house. I thought that would make the transition easier for Ruby."

"How did you feel about giving up your job and moving?"

Anger flared in her eyes. "What are you implying? That I didn't want Ruby?"

"I'm just asking," he said brusquely. "You were on a career path, a good-looking single woman, and now your plans are ruined, and you're saddled with a child to raise."

She lurched up, eyes blazing with rage. But anguish darkened the depths, as well. "I'm not 'saddled with a child,'" she said vehemently. "I would do anything for Ruby. I love her with all my heart."

He wanted to reach out and touch her, calm her. She was trembling so badly that tears spilled down her face again.

"Then come on, Leah." His voice was razor sharp cutting through her, dredging up the guilt. "I know you're hiding something. Do you have any enemies? Maybe an old boyfriend or lover who'd want to hurt you by kidnapping your sister?"

LEAH ALMOST LAUGHED out loud. She hadn't had a boyfriend since high school. And she certainly hadn't had a lover.

Too much guilt and shame from the past had haunted her. And trust didn't come easy. Not after what had happened the night of that horrible party eight years ago.

The party she'd attended in hopes of being with Gage. Only he hadn't shown.

But she didn't intend to tell Gage about that night. It was the deepest, most painful, humiliating, well-guarded secret of her life. Besides, it had nothing to do with Ruby's disappearance.

It was in the past and it had to stay there.

Ruby was all that mattered now. She had to get her back safely. And then she'd never let her out of her sight again.

"Leah?" His voice startled her back to the present. "Is there an old boyfriend or lover who might want to hurt you?"

"No, no one."

"You know something, don't you?"

She lifted her gaze to his. If she discovered a connection, something concrete to make her believe the past was related to Ruby's disappearance, she'd break her promise and tell him. But she'd confronted Charlie when Ruby first went missing and he'd assured her no one would gamble with their futures when she'd kept her vow of silence.

"I told you everything I know," she said, fear making her voice wobble.

A heartbeat of tension passed between them, and her insides churned with worry as he studied her. Then he gave a clipped nod. "The feds put a tap on your phone?"

"Yes, but the kidnapper never called."

"I'm going to hook into your phone, too, just in case. Then I want to talk to your neighbors." He hesitated. "Meanwhile, I want you to take a stab at making a list of anyone you can think of that might have a grudge against you. Anyone with a motive to hurt you or Ruby. Think about your school and the locals—maybe a parent or teacher who paid special attention to Ruby—and even people in Atlanta."

Leah's heart sank. "But I've already been through all this."

"I know, but you might remember something new, even a small detail that might not have seemed significant at the time. How about a woman or man who'd lost a child recently?"

She felt a rush of adrenaline. "There is a woman who lost her daughter a few months ago, a runaway teen." Her gaze swung to his, panicked but hopeful. If this woman had Ruby, she wouldn't harm her. "She always said that Ruby reminded her of her little girl. I didn't think of it before— I felt sorry for her."

"Write down her contact information," Gage said. "I'll check her out along with that father you mentioned earlier."

She nodded, anxious for him to take action. How strange, after all this time, that Gage would come to help her. If he brought Ruby back, she'd more than forgive him for abandoning her that night to her awful fate. She'd forgive everything if it meant having Ruby back, safe and sound.

Chapter Four

Gage looked at the names he'd written down. Dr. Donnie Burkham, the man whose son was bruised, and Carmel Foster, the woman whose daughter had run away.

He'd visit them after he canvassed the neighborhood and stopped by the police station to see just how hard Driscill had searched for Ruby. And to find out if there were any registered sex offenders in the area.

He had to consider all possibilities.

Since it was Saturday, he found most of the ten residents on Leah's street at home. Many of the homeowners were older, empty nesters, and three of the houses were rentals. A Hispanic family occupied one, and a Russian woman with three small children who'd just moved to the area and spoke very little English was renting another one.

The last rental house was empty. The yard was overgrown, the house shrouded in trees. The trash can in back was full, overflowing with pizza boxes and beer cans.

The house backed up to Leah's property Had someone lived there recently or moved out in a hurry?

He jotted down the rental agency. He'd find out who owned the house, who the last renter was and when he moved out. And whether Driscill had bothered to check it out.

He drove into town, passing the Christmas tree lot sponsored by the local Boy Scout troop, noting the sparkling Christmas lights and decorations in the square. The carriage rides offered a quaint tour, past the stores alight with candles and promises of last-minute holiday gift ideas, and carolers serenading children beside the coffeehouse.

On the edge of town, he parked in the gravel lot at the police station, a small, weathered stone building, nearly overrun by untended bushes. Yanking his collar up to ward off the blustery wind, he strode to the door. Brittle grass and pebbles crunched beneath his boots, tree branches swaying violently over his head.

When he opened the door, the scent of strong coffee and stale pastries hit him. He spotted a medium-size paneled room with three desks, one for a receptionist. The other two he assumed were shared by officers.

A pudgy woman with slightly pink hair teased into a bird's nest on top of her head looked up and smiled. "What can I do for you, mister?"

"My name is Gage McDermont. I need to speak to the sheriff."

"McDermont?" She popped her gum. "You related to Jerry McDermont?"

He nodded.

"Well, I'll be damned." She grinned and extended her hand, bloodred fingernails glittering with yellow stars painted on them. How festive.

"My name's Carina Burton. I was two years behind you in school, but I remember watching you on the football field. You were the best kicker Sanctuary High ever had."

He didn't remember her. Then again, he'd only had eyes for Leah.

And if Jerry had been with her, I wouldn't have touched her. We definitely had different tastes in women.

Except for Leah.

Damn. He really thought he'd put that behind him.

"Sheriff's been under the weather," Carina said, "but Charlie's here. He's been in charge about a month now. Running for sheriff in the next election."

Son of a bitch. Just what the town needed, a Driscill monopoly. He'd tangled with Charlie on the football field and off. The guy played to win and didn't care if it was a fair fight or not.

In some ways, Gage was just like him.

But he did what he did to seek justice. Driscill just flat out liked to give a beating. And it didn't matter whether the person deserved it—just depended on Driscill's mood.

Carina gestured for him to follow her down the narrow hallway to another office.

Driscill glanced up from his desk, a look of wary surprise crossing his face. He'd beefed up some since high school, and his hair was shorter now, receding slightly, but Gage would have recognized his tree-trunk neck and crooked nose anywhere. A mean look still glittered in his eyes.

"Gage McDermont, what in the hell are you doing back in Sanctuary? We having a class reunion someone forgot to tell me about?"

Gage forced a chuckle. "Hardly." He shot a look across the office. "I have a feeling you know everything that's going on in this town."

A cocky grin slid across Driscill's face. "It's my job to know." He patted his gun. "And I take my job seriously. What are you doing here, McDermont? I thought you were some hotshot detective in Raleigh."

Gage gritted his teeth. He didn't intend to share the circumstances of his departure from the police department with this moron from his past. "I got tired of playing by the rules and decided to strike out on my own."

Charlie raked a hand over his thinning hair. "You got tired of the rules? Now that's funny. You were always the goody-two-shoes in high school."

He had tried to be the nice guy. But nice guys finished last. "I've changed."

Charlie grinned. "Is that so?"

Gage nodded. "Yeah, I have a private investigation agency. I'm here about Ruby Holden's disappearance."

Driscill's olive skin paled slightly, although he masked his reaction quickly. "You're a P.I. for kids?"

"I'm working for Leah Holden."

Driscill stood, boots hitting the cement floor. "She called you in?"

He shook his head. "I read about the case and heard you'd called off the search, so I offered my assistance. Fill me in. Where are you on the investigation? Do you have any leads?"

Driscill scowled. "If you've followed the news, you know we did everything we could. Organized search parties, questioned everyone in town. Even consulted the feds. But no leads yet."

"Why didn't you immediately call in the bureau?"

"We thought we could handle it ourselves," Driscill said. "Thought the kid just snuck out and got lost or something."

Gage arched a brow. "And the child left that cryptic note?"

A muscle twitched in Driscill's jaw. "We did everything possible to find that little girl. Hell, the whole town was looking for her for days."

"Did you have any viable suspects?" Gage asked.

"No. You know as well as I do that if someone kidnapped her, they're probably long gone by now." He cracked his knuckles. "The feds have issued alerts and have her listed on the database for missing and exploited children. They'll let us know if they get a tip."

"Did you look into that rental house that backs up to Leah's property?" Gage asked.

Charlie frowned. "No. Didn't see a need to."

"The kidnapper could have hid out there."

"Maybe."

"Are there any registered child offenders in the area?"

"Daryl Trevett. I questioned him already and he was working at the plastic factory all night." Charlie lowered his voice. "The problem may be Leah Holden herself."

"What do you mean?"

He cut his eyes toward the door as if debating how much to share, then cleared his throat. "She's had emotional problems. Had a breakdown when her daddy died. That's the reason her mama sent her away her senior year." Driscill narrowed his eyes. "Didn't you know?"

He'd heard rumors.

Driscill shrugged. "Maybe she lost it again when her mama died, and she couldn't handle being a parent."

Gage hid any reaction. He wanted the facts. "You have anything to support that theory?"

"All I know is that she's been seeing a shrink." He jammed a toothpick between his teeth and chewed on it. "And since she moved back, she's kept to herself. Don't want anything to do with her old friends or the town. Except for Jerry, that is. Apparently Jerry thought she wanted to rekindle their relationship."

Jealousy left a bitter taste in Gage's mouth.

Had Leah really tried to get back together with his brother?

HE SWALLOWED THE pill, chasing it with a stiff whiskey, and paced the bottom floor of the old house. The mountains were full of rotting shanties and abandoned houses like this, places he'd discovered on his secret hikes into the woods.

Places no one would think to look because they probably didn't even know about them.

The rooms smelled musty and dank, and he wheezed a labored breath, then removed his inhaler and pressed it over his mouth and nose. Dammit, he was allergic to dust and half the trees in the woods.

Upstairs in the attic room, he heard footsteps. Then the little girl began screaming for help and beating the walls.

A chuckle rumbled in his chest. Poor kid, didn't she know it was futile? They were miles and miles from the town, deep in the ridges.

She could scream her lungs out and no one would hear her.

Sick of her whining, he strode outside to escape the sound. He didn't know what he was going to do with the kid yet.

But Leah Holden had called in the cops, so he couldn't give her back.

Still, he wasn't ready to kill her. Not yet.

If it came down to it, he'd do it. He could bury her out in the hills and no would ever find her or link him to her kidnapping and death.

Then his peaceful life in Sanctuary could go back to normal.

Chapter Five

Leah prayed that Gage McDermont would find her sister. She wondered what he would say if he knew the truth about Ruby's birth.

Nervous sweat beaded on her neck, and she walked over to the mantel and traced a finger over Ruby's Christmas stocking, her heart aching. They'd decorated the stockings together, putting glitter and beads on the white fuzzy edge.

She wanted to see Ruby's face light up when she woke up on Christmas morning and found her stocking overflowing with candy and small gifts. The earrings she wanted. The new markers.

She imagined Ruby scrambling to rip open the packages and play with the kitten that Leah had yet to pick up. She'd chosen a little orange one for her.

What if she never got to give her the kitten? What if Ruby was gone forever?

Dammit, she had to do something. She was going crazy

just waiting. And the more she thought about Charlie Driscill being on the police force, the more distrust rose inside her.

She crossed to the phone book in the kitchen and flipped through until she reached the Ws. She'd try an old friend, the only one from her past that she'd trusted years ago— although she hadn't spoken to him since she'd left high school.

Harry Wiggins. He'd been a science nerd with braces, head of the debate team and a loner, yet she'd befriended him when they'd dissected frogs together in science class. He'd moved back after college and worked as the pharmacist at Sanctuary Drugs. He'd know if Charlie or Evan Rutherford or Jameson Mansfield could be trusted.

She dialed his number, antsy. He'd been on the fringes at the party that night but he hadn't known what was happening to her. If he had, he would have saved her.

The phone rang three, four, five times when finally a woman answered. "Wiggins residence."

Harry's wife, Jeanie. Leah had heard he'd married a woman he'd met at the University of North Carolina. "May I speak to Harry?"

"Who's calling?"

"It's Leah Holden, an old high school acquaintance."

"Oh, hi, Leah. I'm so sorry to hear about your sister. Has there been any word?"

"No," Leah said.

"I'm praying for you. I'll get Harry."

She paced the kitchen while she waited, staring out the window at the bare branches of the tree. They looked as desolate and empty as she felt.

It seemed like an eternity until Harry answered. When he did, his voice sounded low, muffled.

"What's going on, Leah?"

"Harry, I had to talk to you. Ruby has been missing for seven days now."

A long hesitation. "I'm sorry, Leah. I joined in the search party and hated it when they called it off."

"Thanks, Harry." She swallowed hard. "Listen, I wanted to ask if you thought one of the guys from the party that night might have kidnapped Ruby to scare me."

He cleared his throat. "No, Leah. None of us wants to rehash the past. We've grown up, we have families and reputations to protect now."

"That's my point," Leah said.

He sighed. "You haven't given one of them reason to distrust you, have you?"

"You mean have I told anyone what happened?" Disgust ate at her. "No, Harry. I don't want my sister hearing about it."

"Then they'd have no reason to hurt you." He hesitated. "Hang in there, Leah. I'm sure the police will find Ruby."

She bit her lip to stem the tears as she said goodbye. She only hoped Harry was right.

DRISCILL'S COMMENT about Leah being unstable taunted Gage. Did she have emotional problems? Could she have hurt her sister?

He hadn't sensed those vibes from her, but then again she had lied by omission and hadn't told the police or him about her problems.

Questions bombarded him as he drove to Daryl Trevett's house. Granted, Driscill had questioned the ex-con, but he wanted to talk to him in person. He was the obvious suspect—maybe too obvious. He would have been a fool to take Ruby, but pedophiles had compulsions that controlled them.

The trees shook with the force of the wind and somewhere close by a dog barked as Gage parked at the man's rotting old house on the side of the mountain. He knocked on the thin door, scanning the property as he waited. Trevett lived only a few miles from the school where Leah taught, just outside the limit issued by the state.

How many parents in the surrounding neighborhoods knew that a registered sex offender resided within such a short distance of their homes and school?

Possible scenarios flashed through his mind. The man could walk to the school and stalk the children as they came and went, or watch them outside on the playground.

Impatience gnawed at him, and he knocked again, pounding the door. It was dark inside, the lights off as if no one was home. But inside something clattered, then footsteps shuffled.

Finally, the door swung open, and the burly, double-chinned man appeared. A full beard grazed his jaw and his shaggy hair was sticking out in all directions. He was missing two fingers on his right hand, and sported a prison tattoo on the other.

"What do you want?" the man growled.

"Daryl Trevett, my name is Gage McDermont."

"Aww, hell, you're a damn cop."

"No, a private investigator," Gage said between clenched teeth. "And you have a record. Tell me what you know about Ruby Holden."

Anger flared on the man's hard face. "The police already talked to me about her. I don't know nothing."

"Just like you didn't know anything in your trial two years ago about the girl you hurt?"

He cursed. "I was innocent of those charges, and I sure as hell don't deserve to be put under a microscope."

"Is that right?"

"Yeah, that's right." He scrubbed a hand over his beard. "And just for the record, my lawyer is about to get my conviction overturned. The DA withheld some key evidence— the DNA sample that proves I didn't assault that kid."

"A little girl is missing," Gage snarled. "And I don't give a rat's ass if it upsets you to be questioned. I want to find this kid and if you had something to do with her disappearance, I'll see that you go back to the pen."

Trevett bared his teeth. "I didn't take the little girl. I swear." His voice turned low. "I don't like kids, not for sex, not like they said. And my lawyer's going to prove it."

"Then you won't mind me searching your place?"

He gave Gage a glacial look. "Damn right I mind. I had an alibi that night and the sheriff verified it."

"You mind even if it helps prove your innocence?"

"I am innocent, now go to hell."

Trevett slammed the door in Gage's face.

Gage retreated to his car. He'd double check Trevett's alibi and look into that DNA sample.

And then he'd talk to Leah and ask her why she'd lied to him.

LEAH'S FEAR MOUNTED as she waited on Gage to return. She couldn't eat, couldn't think, couldn't do anything but obsess over where Ruby might be.

And whether she was hurting.

Everywhere she turned in the house there were memories, reminders. Photographs of Ruby at the parade on the Fourth of July, of Ruby playing in the sand when they had all vacationed last summer in Wilmington.

Gage's suggestion that she'd missed something—that someone might have been watching Ruby—taunted her, and she retrieved Ruby's backpack. Although the police had been through it before, she decided to check it again.

She rummaged through it, hunting for notes, names, addresses—evidence of anyone Ruby might have been in touch with. In spite of her warnings about strangers, children could be lured into making friends so easily.

Someone could have approached her at school, or even

one of her playmates' family members or neighbors might have befriended her. Someone Ruby would have recognized that night and trusted—the reason she hadn't screamed bloody murder in the middle of the night. Or maybe she had, and Leah had slept right through it.

The thought sent a streak of terror through her again, and she turned the backpack inside out, but found no notes. Just half of a dried-up peanut butter sandwich, some broken crayons, a pencil box and a book of mazes. Ruby liked mazes and unicorns and roller skating and…

More tears clogged her throat, but a knock sounded, so she swallowed them back as she rushed to answer the door.

Gage McDermont. His masculine face was set in a stern frown, his deep-set eyes raking over her.

"What?" she asked in a raspy whisper. "Did you find out something?"

He shook his head, but his eyes looked wary as he entered. "I questioned Trevett. His alibi checked and his lawyer confirmed what he told me—that he's probably going to have his conviction overturned. He didn't assault the kid he was accused of hurting."

She wrapped her arms around herself. Part of her was immensely relieved, but panic set in again because she still had no answers.

"Did you question Dr. Burkham and Carmel Foster?"

"Not yet." He cleared his throat. "I thought you might want to go with me."

She nodded. "All right. Let's go."

"Wait a minute, Leah. I talked to Charlie Driscill."

The blood roared in her ears, and she suddenly swayed, dizzy. "What did he tell you?"

His jaw hardened. "That in high school you had a breakdown and had to be sent away your senior year."

She started to turn away, but he grabbed her arm. She flinched as if he'd hurt her. He quickly let go.

"Listen, Leah, I want to help you," he said gently. "But you have to tell me the truth about what happened. Did you have a breakdown? Why did you go away after your father died?"

Chapter Six

Leah tensed. How could she possibly tell Gage that she'd left town because she was pregnant?

She couldn't. Not when the truth involved his brother. Not when she'd gone to that party to meet him and he hadn't shown up.

She folded her arms across her chest. "Of course. Charlie would say something like that."

Gage narrowed his eyes. "Why would he say it if it weren't true?"

She struggled to reply. "In case you didn't notice, Charlie never liked me."

"He was a badass in high school," Gage admitted. "And he didn't like you because you were smarter than him. He was too busy chasing girls to study."

"I know there were rumors about me leaving town my senior year." She rubbed her arms, suddenly chilled to the bone. "And yes, I did have a difficult time when my father died. My mother thought it would be better if we both got away from the house and all the memories, so we went to live with my aunt in Atlanta that year."

She paused. "And I did see a counselor to deal with my grief but I certainly wasn't in a mental hospital." She forced herself to meet his gaze. "I've also seen a counselor for advice on helping Ruby adjust to losing our mother. If that makes me crazy, then I guess I'm crazy."

"It doesn't make you crazy. Grief is normal." Gage frowned. "Let's go talk to Carmel Foster and Donnie Burkham."

Yes, she wanted—needed—to do something.

"Just let me get dressed."

He nodded, and she hurried toward her bedroom. Charlie had already questioned them but maybe Gage could find out something Charlie hadn't. After all, Charlie had insinuated that *she* had done something to Ruby. That she was unstable and hadn't wanted Ruby.

And the federal agent who'd worked the case, Colby Watson, had been thorough but had also looked at her with suspicion. He'd promised that the feds would still work the case. But so far she'd heard nothing from them. It was as if they'd forgotten Ruby, or written her off as dead.

The more she thought about it, the more she realized that Gage might be the only one who could help her.

WHILE LEAH DRESSED, Gage phoned Agent Colby Watson in Raleigh.

"Agent Watson, this is Gage McDermont." He explained about GAI, and that he was working for Leah Holden. "Did you have any leads?"

Watson cleared his throat. "Not really. We canvassed the town and followed up on the names Ms. Holden gave us. Unfortunately none of them panned out, and every person of interest had an alibi."

He hesitated and Gage heard the sound of papers shuffling. "There was one person—he still worries me. A mentally challenged guy in his early twenties who liked to hang around the park. But we found nothing concrete on him." He sighed. "I didn't want to leave town, but we have a serial-killer case that required me to fly back." He paused. "There was nothing more to do in Sanctuary until we got some leads. We have the girl's photo in all of the databases, and have a tip line for people to call in with information."

"I'll check out the guy," Gage said. "By the way, there's a rental house that backs up to Leah's property. Did you check into who might have leased it lately?"

"No, Driscill said he'd handle it."

"He said he didn't see a need." But Gage did. Someone could have been staking out Leah's place. Maybe they'd left fingerprints. "Tell me, Agent Watson. What did you think about the way Charlie Driscill and his father ran the investigation?"

A tense pause. "The sheriff left things to Charlie, who reacted to my presence the way a lot of small-town cops do. Said he 'didn't need a feebie's help.' But he seemed to cover the bases. They had search teams combing the mountains. He questioned neighbors and other locals." He paused. "I really want to find that little girl. Miss Holden seemed like a nice lady, and she was devastated. Frankly, I'm glad she called in a private investigator. Maybe a fresh set of eyes will see something all of us missed. And I'll do whatever I can to keep the case open until we find her."

"We'll find her," Gage said with conviction. He thanked Watson and hung up just as Leah returned. The vulnerable look in her eyes tore at him, but he steeled himself.

He felt sympathy for the woman. But that was all he could allow himself to feel.

Especially if she had recently tried to pursue a relationship with his brother.

LEAH STARED INTO the deep woods of the mountains as Gage drove toward Donnie Burkham's house.

"The town hasn't changed much since I left," Gage said as they coasted through the town square. "A few more shops, maybe."

"Yeah, the bridal shop is new, and there's a new diner," Leah said as they headed into the mountains. Was Ruby somewhere inside those hills?

"Everyone really rallied together to look for Ruby those first few days. I…have to find a way to thank them sometime."

They lapsed into silence for the next three miles, then Gage veered onto a side road and up the ridge leading to Burkham's estate, a mansion which sat at the top of the ridge with a view of the entire town and surrounding mountains. She stiffened as Gage stopped at the security gate.

Gage punched the intercom button and explained who he was, and the gate slid open. Nerves tightened in Leah's neck as he sped up the drive and parked.

"Looks like Burkham does well for himself," he said as they climbed out.

"Yes. He's a fertility specialist."

Gage rang the doorbell, and a sleek brunette wearing diamonds and a silk suit greeted them. Her smile seemed forced as Gage introduced himself.

The woman shook his hand, then glanced at Leah. "Hello, Leah."

"Mrs. Burkham, I'm investigating Ruby Holden's disappearance."

"The police already talked to us and questioned Donnie," Mrs. Burkham said.

"Is your husband here?" Gage asked.

"No, he's in Raleigh." She frowned at Leah. "I'm really sorry for you and I hope you find your sister, Leah. But you're wrong about Donnie. He didn't hurt our son, and he certainly wouldn't kidnap a child. He's a doctor for goodness' sake—a specialist who helps couples have babies."

"I'm sorry, but I saw bruises," Leah said. "I have to report them, Jane."

"Does your husband have a temper?" Gage asked.

Mrs. Burkham cut her gaze toward him. "Yes, but he's not violent." She walked over to a desk in the corner of the living area, retrieved a folder and handed it to Gage.

"This is a doctor's report on Sammy. He does bruise easily and he's accident prone. We saw a specialist and Sammy has a neurological disorder that causes him to lose his balance. That's why he was bruised, not because Donnie hit him." She sighed and twisted her diamond between her fingers. "Donnie would never hurt a child. Never."

Gage examined the file, and Leah studied the report over his shoulder. Just as Jane Burkham claimed, her son had been diagnosed with a rare disorder.

"I'm sorry to hear this," Leah said sincerely. "Can they help Sammy?"

"They're trying some new medication," Jane said. "That's why Donnie took him to Raleigh, to see a specialist." She gestured toward the door. "Now, if you don't mind, I'd appreciate it if you left."

Leah saw the pain and worry on the woman's face. "I really am sorry," Leah said. "If there's anything I can do—"

"You've done enough," Jane said.

Leah felt her face flush with heat. She'd just made an enemy of the woman but she'd only tried to do what was right for the little boy.

Just as she had for Ruby. She tried not to think about

the fact that Ruby might be safe if Leah had brought her down to Atlanta instead of returning to Sanctuary.

What if she never had another chance to tell Ruby how much she loved her?

GAGE ROLLED HIS SHOULDERS as he climbed into his Explorer. He felt certain he could strike Burkham off his list. He'd dealt with enough domestic cases to believe that Mrs. Burkham and her son weren't being mistreated. Although he could understand why Leah had had to report the incident.

"She hates me now," Leah said. "I guess I can't blame her."

"She doesn't hate you," Gage said. "She's just upset over having to explain things. But you did what you had to do. At least you know the truth about Sammy. And your questions may have prompted them to get him the medical attention he needed."

Leah lapsed into silence as he maneuvered around the winding curves toward the Foster woman's house. He tried not to dwell on the pain in her eyes and the exhaustion lining her delicate face. A week without knowing what had happened to her sister must be killing her.

Unlike Burkham, Carmel Foster lived in a small bungalow in town, a wooden house that desperately needed paint and lawn work. A rusted swing set looked as if it was on its last legs, and a mangy dog sprawled next to the front door.

Gage glanced at Leah. "Are you ready?"

"I hate doing this, knowing what this woman went through."

"Then you don't think she took Ruby?"

"I don't know."

"Let's go talk to her." He climbed out and Leah followed him up to the doorway. A brisk wind rattled the window-panes and dusk had come, casting shadows across the weathered house. He knocked, tapping his foot as he waited. He heard shuffling inside and then the door screeched open.

Carmel Foster was probably in her midthirties, although heavy wrinkles lined her eyes and she reeked of smoke and booze. She spotted Gage and scowled. "What?"

Gage introduced himself. "Ms. Foster, can we come in and talk to you?"

She swept them in with a wave. "I done told the cops I don't know nothing about your sister's disappearance."

Gage scanned the front room, looking for any signs that a child had been there recently. Laundry was piled high on the faded sofa. Two empty liquor bottles sat on the kitchen counter. But he saw no children's clothes in the pile and no hint of food to feed a child on the open shelves.

He inched another step forward and glanced into the bedroom. The covers were rumpled, but the bed was empty. He couldn't see into the other bedroom. "Mind if I take a quick look?"

She frowned but shook her head, and he walked down the short hallway. He looked in the bathroom and saw a child's duck-shaped plastic cup. When he exited, he glanced at the spare bedroom—a girl's room.

Carmel shuffled up behind him. "That's my daughter's

room. She left home a few months ago at fifteen, and I haven't been able to change it since."

Gage turned to stare into her eyes, searching for the truth, but they were glazed with anguish and booze as she looked at her daughter's frilly bed.

Then she turned and shuffled back to the den. "Now you've seen she's not here, why don't you go?"

"I'm sorry, Carmel," Leah said. "But I'm desperate. It's been a week now and there's been no word." Her voice broke. "I'm going crazy with worry."

Carmel's face softened. "I'm sorry, too, Leah. I really am. I know what it's like to lose a child. And I certainly wouldn't will that pain on anyone else."

"You work at the diner," Gage said. "Maybe you heard someone in town talking, or saw someone that looked suspicious?"

Carmel dropped onto the sofa, pushing magazines aside as she settled back and took another swig. "A couple of strangers drifted through a while back, hikers, but they moved on. Only one I can think of that worried me is that weird Warren Cox. He's always lurking around near the playground in the town square."

"Lurking?" Gage asked. "As if he's looking at the children?"

Carmel nodded. "Even though he's in his twenties, he's kind of a kid himself. A big gangly guy. He stutters."

"He's mentally challenged," Leah explained.

Carmel frowned. "Yeah, but he likes little girls."

Leah shivered, and bile rose in Gage's throat. The locals supposedly checked this guy out, but the federal agent had been suspicious of him. Gage would question him himself.

"Thank you, Carmel," he said. "If you think of anything else, let me know." He handed her a business card.

She studied the logo he'd designed for GAI. "You really look for missing children?"

He nodded.

Hope lit her pale hazel eyes. "Maybe when you find Ruby, you can look for my Julie. I have to know what happened to her."

He nodded. "We'll talk when I find Ruby."

She offered a small smile, and he vowed that when the agency was up and running, he'd put someone on her case.

"You really are going to help her, aren't you?" Leah asked as they headed to the car.

"I always do what I say."

She gave him an odd look, emotion darkening her eyes, but she remained silent.

"Let's go talk to Warren," he said. "I want to know just how much this guy likes little girls."

RUBY CRAWLED AROUND the musty attic room, searching for something to use as a weapon in case the mean man came back.

She didn't like him. Didn't want to be here. Didn't believe that Leah didn't want her. They'd cried together when their mama had died, and Leah had promised not to leave her.

Leah read her books at night and told her stories about how she'd dressed like Pippi on Halloween when she was a little girl. Leah baked chocolate-chip cookies and let her stir the dough, and sneak chocolate chips, and they'd strung popcorn on the Christmas tree, and made home-made ornaments from salt dough. Leah had promised they'd make a gingerbread house.

Leah brushed her hair for her at night and sang her to sleep, and cuddled with her in the dark when she got scared of the boogeyman.

Ruby lifted her hand and felt her hair. It was matted and dirty, and hadn't seen a brush in a week. She'd been counting the days by scratching a mark on the wall by the cot. Tears burned her eyes.

Her stomach growled for some of Leah's chicken and dumplings, and she choked back another cry. All the man had given her was peanut butter and jelly sandwiches. She used to like them. Now the smell made her want to gag.

She had to find a way to escape. To find Leah and tell her about the man.

Dropping to her knees, she felt along the wood floor, and her thumb slid over a loose nail in the plank flooring. She practically squealed in glee but pressed her lips together to keep quiet. She didn't want the man to come back.

A splinter jabbed her finger as she clawed at the wood

to pry the nail loose, but she bit back a cry and dug her fingers into the board, twisting and yanking on the nail with all her might. She didn't care how long it took her, she'd pry it free.

And when the man came back, she'd stab him in the eye with it and run until she got so far away he'd never find her.

Chapter Seven

Night was falling by the time Leah followed Gage to his Explorer. Gage's words echoed in Leah's head. *I always do what I say.*

"Really? Is that a new creed of yours?"

His jaw tightened as he looked down at her. "What do you mean by that?"

He hadn't done what he said he was going to do in high school. At least not the night she'd gone to meet him. In fact, his brother had told her that he'd only toyed with her, that he'd never planned to meet her. That he was laughing behind her back.

That was the reason she'd taken that drink from Jerry.

The drink that had knocked her unconscious and made her lose control.

She shuddered. When she'd first awakened the next morning, she hadn't remembered what had happened. But she'd known she'd had sex with someone, and that she'd lost her virginity. Only she couldn't remember the details, and she'd been so ashamed she hadn't told anyone.

Then her nightmares had begun. Gut-wrenching and terrifying with scattered remnants of memories mingled in.

Then her mother had grown suspicious.

She'd been so young and stupid and foolish.

"Leah, what did you mean?"

She shrugged, uncomfortable with the stormy look in his eyes. He almost looked…hurt. "Nothing. I'm just tense and on edge."

His look softened. "I'm trying to help you."

He caught her arm and she felt a sliver of apprehension trickle through her. But it was followed by a sensation she hadn't felt in a long time. A longing to be touched. Held. Loved.

"I know," she said softly. "I guess I'm just surprised."

"Why?"

"I've just been on my own a long time."

And Ruby's disappearance was nothing personal for him. He couldn't know that Ruby might be related to him. Then again, she might not. Leah wasn't sure herself who'd fathered her child.

Only that she'd been conceived that horrible night. But she loved Ruby with all her heart.

"Do you know this guy, Warren?" he asked, oblivious to her turmoil.

She swiped at a drop of perspiration trickling down her

neck, trying to banish the haunting past. Nothing mattered now except finding Ruby.

"I've seen him around town," she said. "He mows lawns and does odd jobs for people."

"Did he ever do any work for you?"

She shook her head. "He came by one day and asked, but I told him that I couldn't afford lawn care."

"Did he talk to Ruby?"

She massaged her temple, battling another headache. "As a matter of fact, when I spotted him, she was in the yard swinging, talking to him. It made me nervous so I went outside."

He gave her an odd look, and her stomach rolled. What if Warren had kidnapped Ruby out of anger or some sick interest in children?

There was really only one way to find out.

GAGE TRIED TO IGNORE the fear in Leah's eyes as he drove through town toward Warren's house, but it was impossible. Her terror for Ruby was palpable.

He also ordered himself to forget the frisson of desire that had rippled through him when he'd touched Leah's arm. He'd liked her years ago—that is, until she'd connected with his brother.

The rivalry between him and Jerry had always been intense but hearing Jerry brag about bedding Leah had cut him to the bone.

That was years ago, he reminded himself. They'd all been young and stupid.

Still, Driscill's comment about Leah calling Jerry nagged at him.

Jerry was married, although Gage had heard that he and his wife were having problems.

And Leah...

He didn't believe Charlie. Didn't think that Leah would try to see a married man.

He stole another look at her. She was suffering now, and he wanted to comfort her. To banish that haunted look from her eyes and bring her sister back to her.

Why hadn't she married by now? She was smart...and sexy, even though she certainly didn't intentionally make an effort to look alluring. She was just naturally beautiful.

"He lives in that trailer with his mother," Leah said, pointing to a double-wide on the hill with a giant plastic blow-up Santa and snowman swaying in the breeze in front. Weeds choked the unkempt yard, and a sagging lean-to built for the old Chevy sat to the right of the mobile home along with a satellite dish.

Gage's tires churned over the graveled drive. "It doesn't look as if he used his yard skills on his own lawn."

Leah clutched the door handle. "I've always tried to be sympathetic toward him, but something about Warren gives me the creeps. If he has Ruby, if he's hurt her..."

He slid a hand over hers and squeezed it gently. "If he kidnapped her, we'll take care of it. I promise."

She turned teary eyes toward him. "I just want her back, Gage. That's all. I just want her back safe and sound."

"I know." Emotions he didn't want to face thickened his throat. He thought about the thirteen-year-old boy he'd lost on the last case and anger knotted his stomach. This case had to turn out differently. "We'll find her, Leah."

She gave him such a trusting, heartfelt look that he almost pulled her into his arms. He forced himself to turn away and get out of the car.

Gage and Leah walked up to the porch and knocked on the metal door. Inside, the sound of country music twanged, and then the door slid open. A woman in her mid-sixties stood in the frame wearing sponge curlers and a faded housedress. "Yeah?"

"Mrs. Cox, I'm Leah Holden," Leah said.

"And I'm Gage McDermont, a private investigator," Gage said. "We're here about Leah's missing sister, Ruby."

"I heard about her. So sorry," Mrs. Cox said. "I knew your mama. She was a good woman. Always kind to me and Warren."

"Thank you," Leah said in a strained voice. "My mother loved this town and all the people in it."

"Mrs. Cox, is your son here?" Gage asked.

She squinted up at him. "He went to take the trash to the dump in the woods. Reckon he'll be back any minute."

Through the kitchen window, Gage spotted the gangly man slogging through the trees in back. "I'm going to talk to him."

"My boy didn't do nothing to Ruby," Mrs. Cox said, her snuff-stained teeth flashing. "He likes kids. He wouldn't hurt one of them."

Gage battled the wind as he stepped outside. Just how much did Warren like kids? He might have the mental age of a child but he had the body of a young man and his hormones might be going crazy.

Leah started to follow him outside, but he said, "Why don't you keep Mrs. Cox company."

She hesitated but nodded, and Warren's mother went to the kitchen to make a pot of tea.

Gage strode down the steps, wanting a chance to talk to Warren alone. What exactly was he doing in those woods?

Dark shadows flickered across the ominous mountains, the thick, dense trees climbing to steep ridges filled with dangers, with abandoned old houses and mine shafts and hundreds of hiding places.

Like a dump in the middle of the woods—the perfect place to bury a body.

LEAH TRIED TO RELAX as Warren's mother brewed tea, but her muscles were in knots. She wanted to know what Gage was saying to Warren.

"I know people are scared of my boy," Mrs. Cox said in a high-pitched tone. "But he's harmless, really."

"I understand you love him." Leah accepted the tea, warming her hands with the mug. "If you don't mind my asking, what happened to Warren?"

Warren's mother claimed an orange vinyl chair at the kitchen table and gestured for Leah to take the chair across from her. "It happened in childbirth," she said with a sad shake of her head.

"I had problems, and he was breech. The doc tried to turn him and then used forceps, but Warren got stuck in the birth canal too long, and, well…he was brain damaged."

"I'm so sorry," Leah said, covering the woman's hand with her own.

"His father couldn't handle having a child that wasn't normal and he left after Warren was born."

Leah gave the woman's hand a squeeze.

"You want me to pray with you now?" Mrs. Cox asked.

Leah looked into the old woman's kind, sincere eyes, hoping that her son wasn't responsible for Ruby's disappearance.

But if he was, she'd make sure he never hurt anyone else again.

Mrs. Cox reached for her hand and Leah accepted it, bowing her head and begging God to send Ruby back before Christmas.

GAGE STUDIED Warren's awkward gait and the childish expression on his face, and pity stirred for him. But he reminded himself that just because Warren was impaired didn't mean that he couldn't have kidnapped Ruby or hurt her.

A skittish look crossed Warren's face, and he paused at

the edge of the woods like a scared colt. His hands were dirty, his shirt stained, his boots marred with mud. He gripped a paper bag in one beefy fist.

"Warren, my name is Gage McDermont. I'm a friend of Leah Holden's."

His deep-set eyes flicked anxiously toward the trailer. "My m…ama…"

"She's inside with Leah."

"Wh…at d…o y…ou want?"

"Leah's sister, Ruby, is still missing. You know her, don't you, Warren?"

"Yeah." He bowed his head. "She's p…retty."

"When did you see her last?"

He swayed back and forth. "I don't re…member days."

"Did you take her from her house?"

Warren kicked his boots on a tree stump, dislodging the mud caked on the sides. "N…o. I told Miss Leah…"

Gage narrowed his eyes. "But you like to hang around the playground in the park, don't you, Warren?"

He shrugged awkwardly, slumped down on the stump, picked up a stick and began to dig the mud from the bottoms of his boots. "Mama d…on't like me trackin' in m…ud."

"Warren, you talk to the little girls at the park?"

He shrugged again. "S…ometimes."

"You ever do anything else with them? Follow them home? Touch them?"

His eyes twitched. "Not follow 'em. Just wanna play with their hair."

"You like playing with the girls' hair?"

"S…oft," he stammered. "But M…ama tell me no." He shook his finger as if imitating his mother. "No touch, Warren. No touch girls. Bad if Warren t…ouch girls."

"Bet that makes you angry, doesn't it, Warren? The girls are so pretty and soft and you want to touch them, don't you?"

He threw a clod of mud onto the ground. "Yes…but M…ama say no. Get mad at me."

Gage squatted down and stared Warren in the eye. "Did you take Ruby from her house so you could play with her hair?"

He shook his shaggy head back and forth. "No…told d…eputy that."

"But you lied to him, didn't you, Warren?" Gage's voice was harsh. If the guy was innocent, he'd apologize later but he had to push for the truth now. "You asked Leah if you could mow her yard and she told you no. Did that make you mad, Warren? Mad enough to sneak back one night and take Ruby to hurt Leah?"

He dug deeper into his shoes, his movements more frantic and agitated. "No, no, no…. Didn't take Ruby."

"You wanted to play with her hair so you took her. What did you do with her, Warren? Did you carry her to a secret hiding place in the woods? Is that where you were now? With Ruby?"

The big man started to cry. He began to rock himself back and forth. "N…o. Been to the d…ump to get pretties."

"Is that where Ruby is? Did you get mad and hurt her, then take her body to the dump?"

"No…no…no!" Warren cried. "No…trash. Not Ruby."

Warren lurched up from the tree stump, swiping at his tears with dirt-stained fingers, hugging his bag to him.

"Show me what you have in that bag," Gage said.

Panic flashed in Warren's eyes, and he shook his head. But Gage reached up and took it from him.

The bag was filled with brightly colored ribbons. Ribbons that looked as if they belonged to little girls.

Bile rose in his throat. He heard footsteps behind him and turned to see Leah approaching, Warren's mother limping behind her.

Warren was wailing now, and Leah looked at Gage in concern. "What's going on?"

"I'm going to call Driscill," he said. "See if he'll get a search warrant for the house as well as dogs to check the dump."

Leah paled as her gaze fell to the bag of ribbons in his hand. "Oh my God," she whispered.

She reached for a pink polka-dotted bow that was hanging out of the bag.

"What is it, Leah?" he asked.

Tears filled her eyes as she looked up at him. "That ribbon belonged to Ruby. I gave it to her for Easter. She used it for her doll, for Matilda's hair."

Chapter Eight

"Warren, where did you get this ribbon?" Leah asked.

He sniffled, looking confused. "I pick them up different places. S...ome in the d...ump. Some in the p...ark."

"How about this one?" She asked again.

"I...don't k...now." He burst into hysterics.

Warren's mother enveloped him into her arms and helped him to the trailer.

Gage phoned Charlie Driscill and explained about the bag of ribbons. Then he asked him to get a search warrant and to send search dogs to the dump.

"I'll take you home, then meet Driscill," Gage said.

Leah shook her head. "No, I'm going with you."

He reached for her hand. "Do you really think that's a good idea, Leah? It may take a while. And you don't know what we'll find."

She swallowed hard, struggling not to allow horrid images of Ruby in the dump to enter her mind. She had to hold on to a thread of hope or she would just curl up and die. "I have to be there," she said. "I just have to."

He squeezed her hand, wanting to pull her into his arms and console her. But time was of the essence. If Ruby was still alive, they needed to hurry. The temperature was dropping by the hour, bad weather threatening.

He coaxed her toward the trailer and inside, but Warren's mother gave Gage an outraged glare. "Just because he has those ribbons don't mean he's a pervert or killer. He likes to collect stuff from the trash, people's yards, the park. And other girls probably had that same color ribbon."

"It had a smudge in the same place Ruby's ribbon did," Leah said.

Mrs. Cox pressed a hand over her chest as if she couldn't breathe, and Leah reached for her.

"Please sit down, Mrs. Cox," she whispered.

"Just look in his room," the woman pleaded. "You'll see all kinds of things he's brought back. He calls them his pretties."

Gage glanced at Leah. "I'll be right back."

But Leah followed him. Warren was crouched on the floor by a black cat, wailing and rocking himself back and forth. Gage bypassed him and went into his room. A baseball spread covered the single iron bed, and a bookshelf overflowed with small rocks, toy cars, trucks and planes as well as soda cans, plastic bottles, ceramic kitties, a stack of sun visors in fluo-rescent colors, and various other items he'd collected.

Gage could be wrong about Warren. But Leah wanted that dump searched anyway.

The only way she would sleep tonight was if she knew that Ruby wasn't in there.

GAGE HAD EXPECTED to find more ribbons, girls' underwear or porn magazines—something more damning than the odd assortment of junk in Warren's room. He searched the closet, beneath the bed and in his boxes of comic books, but found nothing incriminating.

Still, having the ribbons that had belonged to little girls was enough to make the hair on the back of his neck prickle.

A car rumbled up the drive, and he excused himself and went outside to meet the police. Leah followed close behind, hugging her arms around her waist as if she was trying to hold herself together.

Charlie Driscill parked and climbed out. As Gage had requested, he'd brought bloodhounds and two other deputies from the county.

"It's closer if we park on the ridge and go to the dump from there," Charlie suggested.

"We should search the entire area between here and there just in case," Gage said.

Charlie scratched at his thinning hair. "You know you're not in charge here, McDermont."

Gage gritted his teeth. Until he put together his own team of men, he had to have the locals' assistance. "I understand that, Charlie." Gage leaned closer. "But I know you want to solve this case. Just think how impressed your daddy would be."

Charlie stared at Gage without reply. Gage held his ground. Pleasing his father had always been Charlie's weak point, and they both knew it.

Charlie glanced back at the trailer. "I've always thought that nutcase Warren was trouble. If he's a child predator, he sure as hell doesn't belong on the streets of Sanctuary."

The two deputies introduced themselves as Beau Cramer and Jack Rainwater.

"We'll need something of the child's for the dog to sniff," Cramer said.

Gage nodded, and handed him the polka-dotted ribbon. "Will this work?"

Rainwater nodded and took the ribbon. The dogs lowered their heads and sniffed it, then barked and ran toward the woods. Charlie, Gage and Leah followed behind them, jumping over tree stumps and battling branches, shining flashlights and searching the trees and foliage.

Each time one of the hounds paused to sniff a tree or barked and took off running, Leah's face twisted in fear.

His pulse hammered as they approached the dump, and the stench of rotting food and garbage filled the air. He took in the mounds of garbage, broken appliances and discarded furniture, and grimaced. Unlike the city, there were no restrictions on the landfill. At least two miles of trash stretched out in front of them with endless possible hiding places for a body.

He turned to Leah. "I'm going in to search," he said. "Will you be all right?"

She nodded numbly, her eyes glazed with fear, and he fought against offering her false promises. In his job, he'd seen too many bad endings, too much violence and cruelty, to tell her that they'd find Ruby alive.

Not that he didn't hope like hell that they did, that he was wrong and that Warren hadn't done something awful to Ruby and left her here.

Still, either way, Leah needed closure. And if Ruby wasn't here, they'd keep looking until they found her, one way or the other.

He wouldn't rest until Leah had her sister back. Or at least until she knew what had happened to her.

NIGHT HAD SET IN and storm clouds threatened, the dark resurrecting every horror Leah could imagine. The stench of the dump rose in the wind, nauseating with the smell of rotting food, dead animals and God knew what else. Leah covered her mouth, desperate to stifle the odor and control her fear, which was close to bringing her to her knees.

Where was Ruby? Alone and frightened? Fighting for her life?

Or in that trash somewhere, her little body left for an animal to find?

She held her breath as Gage and the men swept flashlights in wide arcs, as they followed the dogs and searched the woods and the endless piles of garbage. She prayed silently that Ruby wasn't in that mess, that they were wrong and Warren hadn't hurt her.

The past few months since she'd moved back to Sanctuary flashed through her head. She'd been apprehensive about her return, had avoided running into people she knew from high school, had contemplated taking Ruby far away so she wouldn't have to face them.

But anger and determination had set in. She'd been running from her past long enough, allowing her nightmares to keep her from coming home to see her mother and Ruby as she should.

She refused to run anymore.

Because Ruby loved Sanctuary. She had friends at school. She loved the mountains and the fresh air and her backyard.

Their house was the only home Ruby had ever known.

How could she move Ruby away from it?

But maybe if she had, Ruby would be with her now. Safe and sound and looking forward to Christmas.

Guilt, worry, regret threatened to overwhelm her. If— no, when—she found Ruby, she had to tell her the truth.

That she was her mother.

That she'd gotten pregnant as a teen. That Leah's mother had insisted on raising Ruby as her child, as Leah's sister—that it would be better for both of them.

Gage stopped to open up a rusted refrigerator. She

cringed, pacing until he looked up at her and shook his head to confirm that Ruby wasn't inside. He seemed attuned to her despair, to know that she needed to be informed every step of the way.

She'd been in love with him when she was young, until that night. After that she'd been ashamed to look at him. And he hadn't exactly pursued her.

Then he'd left for college.

He'd played football for UNC until an injury ended his career. And she'd heard when he'd decided to study criminal investigation and join the police force. Occasionally, she'd even read in the paper about cases he'd solved.

If anyone could find Ruby, he could.

But why was he being so nice to her? Did he know what had happened that night of the party?

Had his brother told him?

Surely not....

No, she refused to believe he knew. Because if he did and hadn't said anything, he was just as bad as the guys who'd slipped the drug into her drink and had sex with her against her will.

If he knew, then her entire opinion of men would be forever tainted.

Who am I kidding? It already has been. That's the very reason I never dated or got involved with anyone in college.

And she wasn't about to start now. She'd protect her secrets. Let Gage help her find Ruby.

And when she had Ruby back, her daughter would be the focus of her life. She'd make up for not acknowledging that Ruby was her child. She didn't care what anyone in Sanctuary thought, not even Gage.

She'd die before she let anyone take Ruby from her again.

GAGE RACED FROM one part of the dump to the other, wielding his flashlight, checking large appliances—a freezer, several refrigerators, a dryer, and then the sofas. He unfolded a hideaway bed, searching the inner cavity, but found it empty.

The dogs sniffed and growled, occasionally locating animal bones, but after hours, they determined that Ruby was not in the dump. The dogs even explored a five-mile radius of the site yet returned with nothing.

Relief swamped him as he conferred with Charlie Driscill and the search team.

"She's not here," Rainwater said. "If Cox killed her, he dumped her body someplace else."

"The river," Gage suggested.

Charlie frowned. "We had a team drag it, but with the racing currents, her body would be long gone."

Frustration and rage made Gage grind his molars. Tomorrow he'd get a map of the area and coordinates for any remote cabins in the foothills. He'd also call the federal agent to see which ones they might have checked out.

He glanced up and saw Leah pacing at the top of the ridge, strain showing on her face.

"I'll let Leah know," he said. "Thanks for all the hard work, you guys."

Cramer nodded and left, but Rainwater hung back.

"What's your next move?" he asked.

"I'm going to get maps of the area and a list of any abandoned houses or cabins where someone might hole up."

"I'd like to help," Rainwater said. "I'm a tracker and I know these woods. Why don't you let me spearhead that?"

Gage studied him, then nodded. "That would really help."

Rainwater nodded. "I'll get on it first thing in the morning."

"Thanks."

Driscill approached, wearing a scowl. "I'll get a court order for a psychologist to evaluate Warren. Maybe he'll confess and we can close this case."

Gage wanted to close it, but he wanted the happy ending. He refrained from comment, not wanting Charlie to know that this case was personal. He nodded, then climbed the hill toward Leah.

She looked so lost and vulnerable that he willed himself not to take her in his arms. Whatever had happened between them years ago didn't matter now. They'd only been kids.

Right now she needed someone to lean on.

She looked up at him as he approached, her pale green eyes haunted and huge in her face. God, he wanted to give her good news.

"She's not there, Leah."

She trembled, biting her lip, tears spilling over. "I was so scared she'd be in there somewhere."

He couldn't resist. He reached out and held her. She collapsed against him, a sob escaping her, and he stroked her back, trying to calm her.

"Where is she, Gage?" she rasped. "It's driving me crazy. Is she cold? Hurt? Alone in the dark? What has he done to her?"

Her voice broke, and he crushed her in his arms, threading his fingers in her hair and wishing he had the answers. Wishing he could alleviate her pain.

Who in the hell had kidnapped the child? Warren Cox? A predator that had long ago left the area?

Or someone in Sanctuary who was watching sadistically now as she suffered?

LEAH CLUNG TO GAGE, emotions churning in heart— Relief. Fear. Despair.

Gage was so strong. He was the rock that she'd never had. She couldn't let go. Finally, she managed to wipe her eyes, and calm herself. "I'm sorry."

"Don't apologize, Leah. I understand how you feel. I want to find her, but I didn't want to find her down there."

Nausea cramped her stomach. "Can we go now? I can't stand the smell any longer."

He guided her up the path to his Explorer, and she settled inside, exhausted. The moon beamed down on the mountain road, the shadows from the trees flickering like a ghost's hands across the black pavement.

Ruby sometimes dreamed of monsters, and Leah had told her they weren't real. She felt like she'd lied to Ruby.

Self-recriminations filled Leah. She felt like the worst mother in the world because she hadn't protected Ruby. "I should have heard when someone came in," she said, her shoulders shaking.

"Don't," Gage said as he started the engine. "It's not your fault. If someone wanted Ruby, they would have found a way whether you woke up or not."

"Is she outside freezing to death?" Leah asked. "Is she tied up, locked in some dark basement, being abused?"

"Leah, stop." He reached over to take her hand but bright headlights suddenly beamed behind them. Gage squinted as the lights bore down on them, blinding him. Tires squealed as the car accelerated.

Leah gripped the door. "What's he doing?"

"I don't know, but he's too close." Gage sped up, but the car raced up behind them, then suddenly tried to pass on the winding road. Gage swerved toward the side of the mountain but the car slammed into his side, and sent the SUV into a tailspin.

Leah screamed and Gage cursed as he tried to right the Explorer. The sedan raced ahead as they skidded toward the ridge, slamming into the guardrail, sparks flying.

The thin metal rail gave way and they careened toward the overhang above the river.

Chapter Nine

Gage sucked in a sharp breath as the SUV finally screeched to a stop, the nose teetering on the edge of the overhang. It was at least a mile down to the river, where water rushed over the jagged rocks. If they went over, they'd never survive.

He glanced at Leah, his hands still wrapped around the steering wheel in a white-knuckled grip. "Are you all right?"

She nodded shakily, shadows framing her pale face. "Who was that?"

Someone who wanted to scare them or someone who wanted them dead? "I don't know. But I intend to find out. Hang on," he said as he started the engine, shifted into Reverse and slowly pressed the gas. The Explorer inched back, tires churning, spewing gravel. He held his breath until they were safely back from the edge of the ridge. Then he checked the deserted, narrow road again, and pulled onto it, heading toward Leah's.

"Sometimes teenagers like to sneak up to Sweetbriar Ridge to park and hang out. That's just ahead."

He shrugged. "Maybe. But I'm going to take paint samples off my car and have them analyzed."

Her breath rushed out. "You don't think it had to do with Ruby, do you?"

"It's possible. But Warren's at the jail right now."

"Maybe Warren is innocent," Leah whispered.

Their gazes locked, the tension between them filled with questions. Leah suddenly turned away, rubbing her arms with her hands.

He wanted to hold her again, to assuage her distress.

She lapsed into silence, both of them warily watching in case the car reappeared and struck again. They passed a truck coming toward them, and two other cars, but the sedan that had hit them seemed to have disappeared into the darkness.

When they arrived at Leah's, he visually assessed the perimeter, looking for anyone lurking around, then walked Leah up to the door. She fumbled with the keys, her hands trembling, and he finally took them from her to unlock the door.

The haunted look in her eyes as she entered the dark, silent house tore at him.

"It's so quiet," she said softly as she flipped on a lamp. "I can hear Ruby laughing in the house. I can see her curled on the floor with that purple comforter watching *Beauty and the Beast*."

"Leah." Unable to help himself, he wrapped his arms around her. She shivered, then leaned against him, obviously physically and emotionally drained. He wondered if she'd slept at all in the last week or if she'd stared into the night, imagining all the horrifying things Ruby might be enduring.

Her sweet feminine scent invaded his nostrils, and her small frame fit perfectly against his hard body. The Christmas tree lights blinked, dappling the adjoining den in a rainbow of colors, reminding him that it was almost Christmas.

"It's been a rough day," he said gently. "Would you like me to get you a drink or something?"

"No. I don't drink," she whispered.

He wondered why, but didn't pursue it.

"It's not what you think," she said quietly. "I'm not an alcoholic. I just don't like to lose control."

He nodded, thinking that was an odd statement. "You need to get some rest."

"I can't sleep," she whispered. "I just lie there wondering where she is. If she's scared or crying for me."

"God, Leah." He kissed her hair, wishing away her pain. But nothing could do that except bringing Ruby home. "We will find her. I promise."

She lifted her head and looked into his eyes, searching, desperate to believe. "I don't know why you came, but I'm glad you're here, Gage. I don't think I could have done this alone."

"You're a strong woman," Gage said.

"I'm just so relieved we didn't find Ruby in that dump. I don't think I could live with that horror."

He cupped her face into his hands. "Listen to me, Leah. You have to be strong, and to think positive. Ruby is going to need you when we find her."

Tears glittered on her blond lashes and she bit her lip as if to control a sob. "I'm trying. It's just so hard."

"I know. But you can do it." The temptation to kiss her overwhelmed him, and he lowered his mouth and brushed her lips with his. She felt so dainty in his arms, so tender, and his own hunger rippled through him.

But her startled gasp made him pull back, and he cursed himself.

He was a selfish bastard. The kiss hadn't been for her, but for him. Hearing the despair in her voice had done something to him, stirring up feelings he didn't want to feel, especially for her.

Hell, he'd just arrived back in town. For all he knew, she had asked his brother back into her life. That's what Charlie had said, anyway.

She stiffened and pulled away, the look of turmoil in her eyes twisting his gut. And there was something else— fear? Was she afraid of him?

"I'm sorry," he said in a low voice as he backed toward the door. "I'll let you know what the doctor says about Warren."

She folded her arms and nodded, a chasm falling

between them. He couldn't shake tension and the unsettling feeling that he had frightened her with his kiss.

Need, hunger, the desire to soothe her—to make love to her—churned through him.

Needs he couldn't pursue.

He laid his business card on the sofa table. "Call my cell if you need me."

Without another word, he turned and left her, cursing himself as he climbed into his SUV and drove toward the rental cabin.

Dammit, he was falling for her again....

LEAH SHIVERED AS she touched her lips where Gage had kissed her.

She hadn't been kissed since…since she could remember. She hadn't wanted a man's touch, or to get close to anyone. But she had wanted him and that terrified her.

Why had he kissed her?

Because he felt sorry for her. That had to be the reason. He was comforting her and she'd read more into it.

Letting him kiss her had been a mistake. One she wouldn't repeat because she couldn't allow a man into her life.

Over the past few years, she'd hated that part of herself. Hated that she'd let those high school boys and what they'd done keep her from wanting to be with a man. The counselor her mother had insisted she see had assured her that those feelings would fade, that one day when she met the right man, she'd overcome her fear. That when she fell in love with someone she trusted, she'd want to be close to him, and she'd enjoy his touch.

But Gage McDermont wasn't that someone. He couldn't be.

She glanced at the phone and noticed the message light blinking. Her heart sputtered and she ran to it, hitting the play button, praying it was news about Ruby, that she'd been found alive and safe.

"Leah, this is Elvira Simmons. I just wanted you to know that we're thinking of you."

She skipped to the next one. "Don't forget about the Christmas Eve service. We're holding a special prayer vigil for Ruby."

Her eyes filled with tears, and she clicked to the next one. "Hi, Leah. It's Danielle's mother, Avery. I have Ruby's costume for the Sunday-school Christmas musical and will drop it off. I just know Ruby will be home by then."

Emotions clogged Leah's throat, and she sifted through the rest of the messages, all from neighbors and Ruby's classmates' parents.

"Where are you, baby?" Leah whispered. "And why haven't I heard anything?"

Battling to hang on to her hope, she bypassed the sparkling Christmas tree, changed into flannel pajamas and went into Ruby's room.

Suddenly outraged and filled with frustration, she dragged Ruby's Christmas robe from the closet and spread it on the bed. Next came Ruby's favorite fuzzy dog slippers, the sweater her mother had knitted for Ruby before she died, the blanket she had given Ruby when she was born. Then she grabbed the Pippi doll and lay down in the middle of Ruby's bed, burying herself in Ruby's favorite things.

Her body shaking, she pressed the robe to her nose and inhaled the scent of Ruby still lingering on the fabric. She pulled Ruby's pillow to her face, hugging the Pipi doll to her as grief overcame her.

She'd never felt so alone in all her life. For a brief second, she wished Gage hadn't left—that he was still there to hold her with those wonderfully strong, comforting arms of his.

GAGE HATED TO leave Leah alone but he had to protect himself.

He went to his rental cabin for a shower, then stopped by the pub and ordered a burger and a beer. It wasn't crowded and he quickly spotted Jerry with some of his old friends at a corner table. Odd that none of them had left town—it was almost as if they were suspended in time, still living out their youthful days, and running the town the way they had run the high school.

In spite of their popularity, they'd been a rough bunch of guys, always in trouble but managing to get away with it. Driscill's father being the sheriff had helped. And Evan Rutherford's and Jameson Mansfield's families had money. Rutherford's grandfather had founded and patented some farming tool that had earned them millions, and Mansfield's father was a powerful attorney who had served on the city council for years.

The only one missing from the crowd tonight was Charlie.

Jerry hadn't noticed Gage yet, so he took a minute to study the group. He noticed Harry Wiggins, who had been a science geek and not part of the in-crowd at the time. It was strange to see him sitting there with Jerry's crowd.

But maybe Gage should cut them some slack. Maybe they'd changed since high school, he thought as he watched them engrossed in close conversation over a pitcher of beer.

Gage had heard Wiggins was the town pharmacist now. Rutherford, the star quarterback, taught history at the high school and had assumed the position of the football coach. He'd become a local legend when he'd taken the team to a county championship. Mansfield had followed in his father's footsteps and attended law school. Now he had a practice in town.

Not yet ready to face them, Gage downed the beer and decided to take the burger with him. But Jerry strode over and claimed the bar seat beside him. "I heard you were in town, Gage."

Gage glanced sideways at his brother, instantly sensing Jerry's animosity. When the McDermonts had taken him in, Jerry had resented Gage's intrusion into the family. He'd never wanted an adopted brother and had undermined

Gage at home, blaming him for any trouble Jerry had started.

When Jerry had acted out, getting arrested for vandalism and drunk driving, the McDermonts had tried to protect him from the law.

"I just got in," Gage said.

"Charlie said you're opening a P.I. agency. What happened to your big-ass career in Raleigh?"

"I wanted a change," Gage said. "Wanted to be my own boss."

"So you came back and finally hooked up with Leah Holden?"

"I didn't hook up with her," Gage said through gritted teeth. Jerry must have talked with Charlie. "She's a client. You are aware her sister is missing?"

"Of course." Jerry shifted sideways. "I helped search just like everyone else in town."

"Do you have any idea who would kidnap Ruby Holden, Jerry?"

Anger flared in Jerry's eyes. "Hell no. What would I know about that slut and her sister?"

Gage squared his shoulders. "She's not a slut, Jerry."

"She was way back when and you know it." Jerry leaned sideways, closer to Gage. "Don't tell me you're still pissed that she picked me over you that night at the party?"

Gage threw some cash down on the bar. "Grow up, Jerry. I'm not revisiting old ground. I've moved on since high school."

"Then go back to Raleigh," Jerry growled. "This is my town, not yours. You never belonged in my family or here. And that Holden bitch certainly isn't worth it."

Gage glared at him with contempt. "I'm not going anywhere, Jerry. Not until I find Ruby Holden and bring her home to her sister." He lowered his voice to a lethal tone. "And when I find whoever took her, I'll see that he rots in jail for the rest of his sorry life."

RUBY WAS DREAMING about being home. Back in her own bed with Leah curled up beside her. It was Christmas Eve and they were baking sugar cookies and decorating them with sprinkles to leave for Santa. Ruby knew Santa wasn't real but she still liked to pretend. So did Leah.

Then she dressed in the angel costume, and Leah helped her strap on the glittery wings. Laughing, they rushed to the church and she joined her friends onstage for the carols.

They'd been practicing for weeks after Sunday school, and all her friends were there, watching.

At the end of the program, the church lights were dimmed and they lit candles and sang "Silent Night." On the last verse, they held their candles high in a sea of flickering white light that was so beautiful Ruby's heart swelled.

Excitement made her jittery. Soon it would be bedtime, and in the morning, she'd find her kitten—

Then something jarred her from sleep, and she clutched her doll, staring into the darkness. Reality crashed in around her and she choked back a sob.

She wasn't home.

And soon it would be Christmas. Unless Leah came for her, she'd miss the musical. Miss baking cookies.

Miss getting her kitten on Christmas morning.

What was Leah doing now? Was she looking for her? Would she find her in time for Christmas?

The squeak of a floorboard suddenly made her still. The man was back. Inside the room.

Fear crowded her throat, and she started to reach for the nail she'd hidden under the mattress, but two large hands pinned her arms and she couldn't move.

A hulking shadow loomed over her, the man's breath smothering her. He smelled like booze and sweat. Then the shiny glint of metal shimmered in the dark.

A gun?

No, scissors....

Cold terror washed over her and she tried to scream, but he clamped a hand over her mouth. "Shut up or I'll kill you."

She shivered as he lowered the scissors and chopped a hank of hair off. Tears filled her eyes, and she held her breath, willing him to leave. She didn't want him in the room.

Didn't want to die.

Then his feet pounded the wood floor as he left the room. The screech of the door locking swept her back into the darkness.

She slammed her fists against the wall. "You're a bad man, and I hate you!" she screamed.

His laughter boomeranged from the hall through the eaves. She pressed her hands over her ears to drown out the ugly sound.

LEAH JERKED AWAKE to the phone ringing. She fumbled in the dark, clawing her way up from the bed and racing to the den. Her heart was pounding, the blood roaring in her ears. Was it Gage with news about Ruby?

Shoving a tangled mop of hair from her eyes, she cleared her throat. "Hello?"

"You want to see your sister again?"

She frowned at the mechanical-sounding voice. "Where is she? Is she all right? Can I talk to her?"

"Get rid of the P.I. If you don't, Ruby is dead."

Chapter Ten

Gage tossed and turned all night, memories of Jerry flashing through his head.

Why did Jerry still have such animosity toward him?

And why had he called Leah a slut?

In high school, Jerry had bragged about sleeping with girls. But as he'd done with most of them, once Jerry had conquered Leah, he moved on to another.

By dawn, frustration knotted his shoulders. Gage threw the covers aside, pulled on some shorts and headed into the woods for a five-mile run. When he returned, he showered and hit the coffeepot, anxious to get started with the day.

He scraped the sedan's black paint off his Explorer from the sideswipe the night before, and sent it to a private lab for testing.

Then he phoned the real estate agency, located the owner of the rental house and learned the house had supposedly been empty for a month. He got the woman's permission to search it, then asked her to send him a list of any vacant cabins or houses in the woods that were for sale or rent so he could check them out.

When she faxed it to him, he looked it over and then faxed it to Rainwater, not caring if he pissed off Charlie Driscill, whom he had finally convinced to meet him at the rental house behind Leah's with a crime unit. He wanted to go over the place with a fine-tooth comb.

The kidnapper could have moved in, stalked Leah and slipped out through the woods between the properties to take Ruby. If they were lucky, he had left prints.

Then Gage could nail his ass to the wall.

As he drove to the rental house, he passed Leah's, wondering if she'd slept at all. If she'd lain awake all night worrying about Ruby.

If she'd even thought about that kiss…

That damn kiss had haunted him all night. The feel of her lips on his. The taste of her sweetness. The fact that he'd wanted to kiss her years ago but had never gotten up the nerve.

Dammit. He'd kissed a lot of women in his time. Slept with a few although he wasn't the kind of guy who went out looking for a one-night stand. In truth, he'd never been good at that. He'd always wanted more.

His childhood had played a part in his attitude, as well. Having been tossed away by his mother and never having known his father, and then living in the orphanage, he'd craved stability. A normal home life. A loving family.

And now, a woman to settle down with, one who'd be faithful and love him back.

He'd thought he'd found stability and love with the McDermonts when they'd adopted him. He'd been thrilled about having a younger brother so close in age.

But Jerry had resented the hell out of his presence and had tried to make his life miserable.

By high school, Gage had learned to steer clear of him. To take what attention the McDermonts gave him, and accept that Jerry and he would never be close.

But he'd wanted to make the McDermonts proud.

That was one reason he hadn't slept with every girl who'd hit on him and bragged about it like the other guys in the locker room.

Leah was another. He'd had a thing for Leah because she seemed like a nice, genuine girl. She was quiet, shy, studious, and not a big flirt like some of the others.

But she'd chosen Jerry that night and it had stuck in his craw like nothing else ever had. He'd been furious and decided if she wanted to hang with the bad guys, that was her choice.

Hell, that was eight years ago. Kids made mistakes. Why did it still matter now? They were adults.

He parked in front of the rental house and waited on Charlie and the crime unit. When Driscill arrived, his eyes looked bloodshot, as if he hadn't slept, and his hair looked disheveled. "This is probably a waste of time."

"It's worth checking out," Gage said.

The crime unit, a male and female CSI, went inside to process the house. Gage canvassed the outside of the ranch structure, searching for anything that might point to a former tenant or poacher.

No toys left behind or yard tools. But he spotted an old pie tin shoved beneath the steps and decided to have forensics check it out. Using his handkerchief, he picked it up and smelled it. Dog food.

Had the former tenants owned a dog? Or could someone have stayed in the house and kept a pet there—maybe a puppy they'd used to lure Ruby out of her house that night? It was the perfect ploy to trap a child.

He carried the pie tin inside the house. The scent of bleach assaulted him the moment he entered. Someone had cleaned the place. Perhaps to erase evidence of a crime.

Would the investigators be able to find anything or had the tenants wiped away any trace of themselves?

Another question niggled at the back of his mind. When had the house been cleaned?

Had someone in town discovered he was going to have it processed and gotten there first?

LEAH KNEW WHAT she had to do. Call Gage and tell him to stop investigating. To leave her alone.

Then maybe she'd get Ruby back.

Or was the kidnapper toying with her? Trying to torment her with hope so he could buy some time to escape?

The Christmas tree with Ruby's presents beneath it mocked her from the living room. Ruby had to be home for Christmas....

If Warren hadn't kidnapped her, who had?

She crossed to the sofa table and picked up Gage's card.

A manila envelope on the floor in front of the door caught her eye. Her heart stopped as she knelt to retrieve it.

She flipped it over with shaking hands, searching for a name or address, even a postage stamp to show where it had been mailed from, but it was blank. Maybe the kidnapper had slipped it under the door with some demands or instructions where to find Ruby. Which meant he was still close by, in town.

Her heart started up again, racing, drumming against her breastbone as she tore open the envelope. Inside she found a small white business envelope.

A piece of hair was inside. Strawberry-blond hair—Ruby's.

She removed a plain piece of computer paper and bile rose in her throat.

It was a note.

DO AS I SAID OR NEXT TIME IT WILL BE A FINGER.

GAGE WANTED TO GO check on Leah but he followed Charlie back to the police station. The psychiatrist from Sanctuary Hospital was waiting when they arrived, and introduced himself as Dr. Roscoe Jennings. He was fit and well groomed, with slate-gray, probing eyes and silver-tipped hair. Gage guessed his age to be midfifties.

"I understand he's a suspect in the child kidnapping," Dr. Jennings said.

Charlie nodded. "Yes, sir. He has some mental disabilities, and likes to hang around the park and watch the kids."

Dr. Jennings's eyebrows rose. "I see. All right. Let me talk to him and I'll give you my opinion."

Deputy Cramer appeared from the back, rubbing his head. "That psycho has been wailing like a damn baby all night." He grabbed his hat. "I'm going home to grab some shut-eye."

Charlie nodded, and Dr. Jennings's mouth tightened as he and Gage followed Charlie through the double doors down a narrow, dark hall to a cell. Warren's wails echoed off the stone walls. He sounded like an injured animal, his cries not human.

When they reached the cell, Gage fisted his hands in frustration. Warren lay on the cot in a fetal ball, screeching and crying. He didn't know if they'd get answers or not.

"Open the door," Dr. Jennings said to Charlie.

Charlie removed the keys from his belt and jammed one in the cell door, then swung the barred door open. Dr. Jennings walked inside, his expression concerned.

"Warren, my name is Dr. Jennings," he said in a low, soothing voice. "I'd like to talk to you."

He approached him slowly, then placed a hand on Warren's shoulder and patted his back. "Please, stop crying and talk to me? I'm not here to hurt you. I want to help you."

Gage clenched his jaw, trying to be patient with the sobbing man. If Warren *had* hurt Ruby, he obviously had a conscience. But he was so childlike that Gage couldn't see Warren intentionally hurting anyone.

It took several more minutes of Jennings's gentle coaching before the big, gawky guy unrolled himself and sat up. Bruises marked his forehead and hands, and Dr. Jennings jerked his head toward Charlie, pinning him with an accusatory stare.

"What happened to him?"

Charlie shrugged. "He was upset when we locked him up. Banged his damn head and fists against the wall."

"I'm having him transferred to the hospital for evaluation," Dr. Jennings said. "He needs medical care and sedation."

Warren stared, glassy eyed, at them, his body shaking. "D...idn't do nothing," he whimpered. "D...idn't h...hurt R...uby."

"It's all right, Warren," Dr. Jennings said. "I'm going to call your mother and we'll take care of you."

"D...idn't hurt her," Warren said again. "'D...on't touch the girls,' Mama says. Do what Mama says."

"Don't tell me you believe this nut?" Charlie mumbled.

Dr. Jennings glared at Charlie again. "He doesn't belong here. Phone his mother and tell her where we're taking him."

Dr. Jennings patted Warren again. "I'll be right back, Warren." He called the hospital for an ambulance to transfer Warren to the psychiatric ward.

Gage grimaced. He had to trust that Jennings knew what he was doing and that he'd get the truth from Warren.

Considering Warren's mental state, if he had taken Ruby, he would have broken and confessed after a night in jail. He was nothing more than a child in a man's body. He didn't have the intelligence to pull off a kidnapping scheme and keep quiet about it.

Dammit. Gage had hoped they'd have some answers by now. Who had abducted the little girl?

Maybe forensics would find something at that rental house.

His cell phone trilled, and he checked the number. Leah. He gritted his teeth, wishing he had more to tell her.

LEAH'S HAND SHOOK as she placed the manila envelope holding the note and Ruby's hair on the kitchen table.

The phone clicked. "It's Gage."

"Gage…"

"Listen, Leah, I'm coming over there right now."

"No, Gage, that's the reason I called. I…don't want to see you anymore."

"What?"

"I want you off the case."

A tense moment passed before he replied. "I'll be right there."

"No—"

But the phone went dead. She closed her eyes, bracing herself to lie and do whatever she had to do to get rid of him.

Frantic with fear, she hurriedly threw on some jeans and a sweater, then paced the den floor, glancing at Ruby's Christmas stocking on the fireplace, her head spinning. Was she doing the right thing by firing Gage? So far, he'd taken more interest in finding Ruby than the local cops.

But the note haunted her.

DO AS I SAID OR NEXT TIME IT WILL BE A FINGER.

She couldn't let this maniac hurt Ruby.

And he had to be watching her or he wouldn't know Gage was working with her.

Ten grueling minutes later, a knock sounded on the door, loud and pounding. "Leah, open up. It's Gage."

She swallowed hard, gathering her courage as she strode to the door and opened it. Gage's startling dark eyes pinned her, then he pushed his way inside.

"What's going on, Leah?"

She licked her dry lips. "What did you find out from Warren?"

His eyes narrowed as a muscle worked in his broad jaw. "Nothing. Dr. Jennings, the psychiatrist who came for the evaluation, moved him to the hospital. His mother is meeting him there and he's going to sedate Warren and hope that he talks."

Fear strained her breathing. "He didn't say anything?"

"He insists that he didn't hurt Ruby."

"Do you believe him?"

He shrugged. "I'm not sure, but maybe. If he hurt her,

it was accidental. The kidnapper has very little conscience or he wouldn't have abducted a child, especially at the holidays." He hesitated. "Warren doesn't seem to have a vindictive bone in his body. He's too…childlike and wants to please his mother. The guilt would have driven him to a confession."

Leah bit her lip to stem her disappointment and turned away. In her heart, she had sensed that Warren was innocent—and how could he have delivered that note if he was in jail all night?

"Talk to me, Leah." Gage moved up behind her, and rubbed her arms with his big hands. Masculine hands but they were so gentle, his tone so caring that she wanted to fall into his arms.

Still the warning taunted her. "I need you to leave, to stop investigating."

"Why?" he asked in a gruff voice. "You want to find Ruby, don't you?"

"Yes, God, more than anything." Her voice wavered. "But I don't want you on the case anymore."

He spun her around, anger flashing in his eyes. The heat between them was intense, the tension palpable. "Is this because I kissed you, Leah?"

Her chest ached from holding back her tears. And the truth. She'd liked the kiss, wanted his comfort. *I've been so alone for so long.…*

"No." She tried to pull away, but he held her firmly in his grasp.

"It is, isn't it? Why, Leah?"

"I don't want to discuss it," Leah said. "I just want you to go, Gage. To leave me alone."

"You're frightened of me, aren't you?"

Yes, she was afraid. He made her feel things she'd never felt for a man. He made her want to be normal again. To be kissed and held and loved.

But she had to think of Ruby. Ruby came first in her life. She always would.

"I just need for you to leave me alone." She jerked away, forcing herself to be strong, gesturing toward the door. "Now, please go, Gage. The police will help me."

His sardonic laugh echoed in the room. "You don't really believe Charlie Driscill is doing all he can do to find Ruby and neither do I. He's doing the minimum, just covering his own ass to please his old man." He lifted her chin and forced her to look into his eyes.

"Level with me, Leah. If it's about me kissing you, it won't happen again. But let me find Ruby."

She felt herself crumbling, felt her legs go weak and her knees buckle. A sob welled in her chest, escaping in a painful rush.

Her voice came out a choked whisper. "You don't understand, Gage, he's watching. And he's going to hurt Ruby if you stay."

Chapter Eleven

Gage caught Leah as her body swayed and a cry tore from her, his heart hammering in his chest.

"What are you talking about, Leah?"

She sagged against him, a bundle of pain. "They'll hurt her if you don't drop the investigation."

Her words slowly registered, and he quickly realized her meaning. "You heard from the kidnapper. He threatened you, didn't he?"

She nodded against his chest, and he wrapped his arms around her, crushing her in his embrace. "Leah, talk to me. I'm here to help, not cause you more distress."

"He called." She shuddered against him, clinging to his arms, her pain so intense he felt it in his bones. "And this morning, I found the note…"

He stroked her back, desperate to calm her. "What note?"

"A warning and a piece of Ruby's hair." Her voice cracked, and she clung to him, her body trembling.

Concern for her welled in his chest, along with fear.

In light of this information, the sideswiping incident the night before seemed more ominous. It might not have been accidental, or just a case of teenagers gone wild. Maybe it had been intentional, meant to stop him and Leah from uncovering the truth.

Unable to resist, he pressed a gentle kiss to her hair, inhaling her shampoo and the sweetness of her skin. She made him want to soothe her pain and promise to protect her forever. Leah was soft and loving—and utterly scared out of her mind.

"Leah, tell me exactly what happened. What did the caller say, word for word?"

"That he'd warned me," she whispered raggedly.

He massaged her shoulders with one hand, cradling her against him with the other. "I want to see the envelope with the note and hair."

She gulped in a breath, then lifted her head and scraped the hair from her damp cheek. He reluctantly released her, missing her body as she crossed to the kitchen and gathered a manila envelope.

He mentally braced himself as he used his handkerchief to take the envelope from her trembling hands.

A cold wave of fury washed through his veins when he discovered the lock of hair. Then he read the note and cursed.

The kidnapper wanted her to get rid of him. Well, too damn bad.

"Look at me, Leah."

She wiped her tears then finally met his gaze.

"I left the force so I wouldn't have to play by the rules. And I'm not giving up on this case now."

THE IMPLICATION OF Gage's words should have terrified Leah, but for the first time since this nightmare began, a small semblance of hope flared inside her. She wasn't alone. Someone was on her side. Someone who'd fight until he brought Ruby home.

But the warning and the note taunted her. What if she was wrong? What if, by letting him stay, she caused this crazy man to do something horrible to her little girl?

"I couldn't live with myself if he hurt her," she whispered.

"This guy wants to scare you, and I'm guessing he wants a way out. We'll figure out how to give it to him, or find him first."

Gage placed the note back inside the envelope. "I'm going to send this to the lab. Maybe there's a print on it. And the handwriting expert can analyze the writing."

She nodded.

"You didn't recognize the caller's voice last night?"

"No. It sounded odd, like a mechanical voice."

"How long was he on the phone?"

"Just a second."

"Not long enough to trace. But all your calls are still being recorded, aren't they?"

She nodded. He went to the machine the police had installed and listened to the cryptic message. "I'm going to send this tape over to the lab, as well." He removed the small tape and replaced it with another.

"Get your jacket, and let's go for lunch. Then I'll take care of this."

"I'm not hungry," Leah said.

"Come on, Leah, it'll do you good to get out."

Panic flickered in her eyes. "But what if he calls while I'm out? Or what if he's in town and sees us together? Then he'll know you're still here."

"Then we study people's reactions to us. That might lead us to this guy."

Maybe he was right. She went to the closet, grabbed her denim jacket and followed him outside, glancing around her to see if anyone might be watching.

"This kidnapper is cunning," Gage said as they got in his Explorer. "The kidnapping was premeditated, Leah. It was not the random act of a pedophile." He started the engine and drove toward town. "The fact that someone hand-delivered this envelope means he's probably a local and probably still in town."

His gaze cut to hers. "This also sounds personal. He took a chance on coming to your house to deliver this. It may be someone you know."

A cold knot of fear tied her stomach into knots. "Someone who lives in Sanctuary?"

"Someone who has something against you," he said quietly.

As in someone who didn't want her back in town?

Maybe she'd been crazy to believe that Charlie and Evan and Jameson could be trusted.

GAGE SAW LEAH'S face pale. But for a brief moment something flashed in her eyes, some seed of suspicion, as if his words had struck home.

"You're thinking of someone, aren't you?"

He parked at the jail, and Leah's gaze shot to the building.

"Leah, if you suspect someone, why won't you tell me?"

Charlie Driscill drove up in the squad car and climbed out. Leah's face became neutral.

Dammit. Every time he thought he'd gotten closer to her, she shut down. "Let me give this to Driscill for CSI to process."

Charlie met him at the car, one hand resting on his weapon as if he liked the feel of the gun in his holster. Some cops fed on power. Was Charlie one of those?

Gage grabbed the envelope, stepped from the car and explained to Charlie about the contents. "Will you have CSI pick it up and analyze the tape, envelope and contents?"

Driscill nodded. "Sure." He glanced at Leah and flicked his hand up in greeting.

"Don't let it out of your sight," Gage said. "This could be our first lead. And we'll need it as evidence when we catch this guy and send him to trial."

If Gage let him live long enough to make it to court.

When he settled back in the car, Leah averted her gaze, deep in thought. A strained silence fell between them as he drove to Delilah's Diner, and they went inside.

It still looked the same inside except, in light of the holiday, Christmas music filled the cozy room instead of country tunes. Red-checked tablecloths covered the tables, booths lined the walls and photos of the mountains and nearby waterfalls covered the pine paneling.

A large jar for donations to Magnolia Manor—the orphanage where Gage had spent several months before going to live with the McDermonts—sat on the counter near the old-fashioned cash register. A Christmas tree decorated with birds' nests occupied the space beside it. A few presents lay beneath it for the kids at Magnolia Manor.

Delilah waddled over, the lights on her green Christmas sweater twinkling, a pencil stuck in her teased, platinum-blond hair. "Why, Gage McDermont, I heard you were back in town, boy." She clucked her teeth, then whistled as she looked up and down. "You've done growed into one fine-looking man." She glanced at Leah. "Don't you think so, honey?"

Gage grinned and hugged Delilah, but Leah was silent.

"What is it, Sugar?" Delilah said to Leah. "He so smokin' he done got you all tongue-tied?"

"He's working for me," Leah said stiffly. "Trying to help me find Ruby."

"Oh, Lordy, baby. I'm sorry. I didn't mean to be insensitive." Delilah's smile faded. "I've been praying for you and her."

Leah nodded and stared at the menu as if she wanted to escape. Gage ordered the special of the day, Delilah's meatloaf. Leah ordered a cup of soup and sweet iced tea.

"Tell me about Ruby," he said. "What's she like?"

A light sparkled in Leah's eyes as she thought for a moment. "She likes to roller skate and ride her bike and draw." She traced a water droplet on the glass. "She's a pretty good little artist, but she can be a tomboy, too."

Delilah brought their food and he dug in while Leah only took small spoonfuls of soup.

"Ruby sounds like you," he said, remembering that Leah had worked on the yearbook staff and run track.

An odd look flickered across her face. "She wants a kitten for Christmas," Leah said, sadness back in her voice. "I have one on hold, a little orange furball with big ears."

He covered her hand with his, and she curled her fingers into his palm. "You'll give it to her," he said quietly.

The bell on the door jangled, and he glanced up and saw his brother enter. Jerry's gaze met his, his mouth tightening as he spotted them together. Then he shocked Gabe by walking over to them.

Leah jerked her hand from his and gripped her tea glass. Gage frowned. Did she not want Jerry to see them together?

"Well, well, if it isn't my brother and Leah Holden together." Jerry pulled at his chin. "I thought you were leaving town, Gage."

Leah stared into her tea, and Gage glared at Jerry. "No, still establishing my investigative agency and looking for Ruby Holden."

A vein pulsed in Jerry's forehead, and his eyes looked as if he'd had too much to drink the night before.

"Found anything?" Jerry asked.

"Maybe." Gage wasn't about to give him any information. His cell phone rang and he checked the number. His friend from the crime lab. He hated to leave Leah alone with Jerry, but the call could be important. "I'll be right back. I need to take this."

He stood and walked to the back by the restroom, keeping an eye on the table as he connected the call. "McDermont."

"Gage, we found a partial print on that dog pan along with a human hair. I ran it through the system but didn't get a match. But if you find the guy, we can probably use it."

"Thanks. I appreciate your letting me know."

Jerry leaned closer to Leah, then grasped her arm and said something in her ear. She responded in a hushed voice and Jerry laughed. What were they talking about?

Was something really going on with Leah and his brother?

LEAH JERKED AWAY from Jerry. "Leave me alone."

"What are you doing with Gage, Leah?" Jerry said.

"He's helping me look for Ruby. Do you know anything about her disappearance, Jerry?"

"Hell no. Why? You haven't broken your promise, have you?"

Gage appeared and cleared his throat. When Leah glanced up, he was staring at them, at Jerry's hand on her arm, his expression colder than she'd ever seen it.

Jerry grinned then straightened. "Good luck finding the kid." He went to the counter, paid for a to-go order and left.

Leah was trembling as she watched him leave.

"What's going on between you and my brother?" Gage asked.

Stunned at the anger in his voice, she fidgeted, struggling for a reply. "Nothing." She stood, irritated with Jerry. "Will you please take me home now?"

He nodded, dropped some cash on the table for the bill, then followed her to the door. Outside, a wind whipped her hair in her face, and she shivered, pulling her jacket tighter around her as she looked up into the tall mountain ridges.

Gage had suggested that someone in town wanted to hurt her. At least four people were displeased that she'd returned to Sanctuary. Maybe it was time she swallowed her pride and told Gage. After all, they'd exhausted all the other possibilities.

Gage slammed the car door and drove in silence to her house. But instead of leaving her at the door, he followed her inside.

"All right, Leah, enough games. Are you seeing my brother?"

Shock rolled through her and she spun around to him.

"Good heavens, no. Why would you suggest a thing like that?"

"I saw him touching you," Gage said tightly. "And you two were whispering."

Nausea rippled through her and she crossed to the kitchen window. She imagined Ruby swinging in the tire swing and her heart clenched.

"Leah," Gage said in a gruff voice. "I know what happened back in high school."

She sucked in a sharp, painful breath, unable to face him. "What do you mean?"

"He told me."

She swung around, balling her hands into fists. "Jerry told you about that night at the party?"

His look darkened. "Yes."

Rage clawed at her, and she lunged toward him and hit him with her fist. He'd known and he hadn't done anything. He had kept the nasty secret just like the others. She'd thought he was different and had trusted him.

She'd let him comfort her and hold her. And she'd liked that kiss.

He must think she was pathetic.

"Get out, Gage." She shoved him backward with her hands. "Get out and don't come back!"

"What?"

All the stress and fear of the last few days welled into a giant mass of fury. "I hate you," she said. "You heard me. Leave and don't ever come back."

HE PULLED HIS COAT up around his neck, cursing at the bitter cold as he watched Leah's house through the binoculars. He hated her for what she'd done to him. Turned him into a damn Peeping Tom when he should be warm and content at home sipping his favorite scotch by the fire.

Damn. He'd never thought it would come to this. He thought his life was going perfectly.

Now everything was falling apart.

And it was all Leah's fault.

She was cozy with the bastard McDermont. Was she sleeping with him now? Spreading her legs and welcoming him inside her body when she'd shunned him for years. When she'd tried to push him away as if he wasn't good enough for her.

Hate rose in his gut, burning as hot as the fire.

McDermont had found that rental house and the stupid dog bowl. Would he find a print on it?

If so, he'd put two and two together and discover he'd taken the kid.

Maybe he should just get rid of her permanently.

He gripped the binoculars with sweaty fingers, tense as he contemplated what to do.

He'd never thought he could kill another person.

But his future was at stake.

And he loved this town. It was *his* town, by God, and he wouldn't let her run him out or send him to jail.

Yes, he'd take care of Leah. She posed the real danger. So did McDermont. Maybe he'd kill them both and make it look as if Leah had killed McDermont and then offed herself.

Then he'd decide what to do with the kid. After all, she hadn't seen his face and couldn't identify him.

But Leah—she had to die.

Then he'd go on with his life in Sanctuary exactly the way he'd planned.

Chapter Twelve

Gage's head rang with confusion. What in the hell?

Leah shoved at him, beating him with her fists. "Get out!"

He grabbed her wrists to keep her from hitting him again, shocked at her outburst. He'd seen her upset before but nothing like the cold rage darkening her eyes now. "Leah, what's going on?"

"You knew all these years and you never said anything." A sob burst from her, so deep and anguished that it tore at him. "I thought you were different, not like them. I let you in here and…God, I'm going to be sick."

She suddenly turned and ran to the bathroom, slamming the door.

His heart pounded. Something was wrong. Very, very wrong.

A cold knot of dread gripped him as he walked to the bathroom door. The sound of her retching echoed from inside. Sweat beaded on his skin, and he opened the door and found her on her knees, crying as she propped her head on the toilet.

He grabbed a washcloth from the towel bar, dampened it with cold water and pushed it into her hands.

"Go away," she cried. "Please go away."

"I'm not going anywhere," he stated emphatically. "Not until you tell me what in the hell that was all about."

"No, just get out of here," she cried. "I can't stand to look at you."

Her words cut razor sharp like a knife, but he reached for her.

She shoved his hands away.

"Leah, you have to talk to me."

She wiped her mouth, then stood, gripping the sink to support herself. He stepped back into the doorway to give her room, and she splashed cold water on her face and rinsed her mouth with mouthwash.

Still leaning against the sink, she looked up at him in the mirror, hate, despair and desperation in her eyes. "I can't believe I trusted you. You've known all these years. Did you come here pretending to want to help me find Ruby just to spy on me? To make sure I kept quiet to protect your brother?"

His lungs tightened as that feeling of dread began to overwhelm him. "Protect my brother from what?"

"From me breaking that vow of silence."

Her tone sent fear down his spine. She stormed past him and back to the kitchen. Then she dropped down into a chair and put her head in her hands.

His pulse raced furiously as he sat down beside her, and he inhaled sharply to control his reaction, which ping-ponged between cold fear and fury. "In case you haven't noticed, Jerry and I aren't exactly close. In fact, we've hardly spoken since high school."

She frowned. "You said he told you—"

"The night of the party, the one I asked you to come to, he called me and told me that you came, but that you wanted to be with him, not me. That's why I didn't show up."

Her eyes widened in shock as she turned toward him. "What?"

He ground his teeth. "You heard me. I asked you to meet me, but Jerry called and said you'd only come to see him. Then he bragged the next day that he slept with you. I hit him and we got into a fight." He balled his hands into fists now, the memory making him shake with anger.

She buried her head in her hands again.

"Are you telling me that isn't what happened? That you didn't choose him over me?"

He held his breath while he waited on her reply. But he saw the truth in her pain-filled eyes when she looked at him, and rage unlike anything he'd ever felt churned inside him.

"Leah," he said in a hoarse voice. "Tell me the truth."

She pressed a hand to her mouth, a strained silence passing between them as if someone had died. Finally she inhaled a deep breath and dropped her hand. "I didn't choose him that night," she whispered. "I d…idn't choose at all."

He closed his eyes as the reality sank in. So Charlie had lied to him. Leah hadn't wanted to renew a relationship with Jerry.

LEAH WAS TREMBLING, the past few minutes taking their toll. She'd hated him with every fiber of her being because she'd trusted him, the first man in years she'd even considered allowing to touch her.

Had Gage really not known the truth? Had he believed she'd chosen Jerry over him?

"Tell me everything," he said, his jaw clenched.

She shook her head, uncertain if she could voice the ugly words. The only people she'd ever told were her mother and the counselor.

"Leah, please."

His voice sounded gruff, choked with shock and anger. Jerry had obviously lied to him, just as he'd lied to her.

"I have to know what happened," he said.

She couldn't look at him, so she stared at her hands in her lap. She needed a manicure, she thought insanely. And her hands were dry and chapped.

She looked up at his hands—masculine and strong. They had comforted her. She had to tell him.

"I did go to the party," she finally said in a whisper. "But I came to see you. I had such a crush on you back then. I couldn't believe you wanted to be with me."

He'd be repulsed when she finished her story, but she was

beginning to think that Jerry or one of the others had stolen Ruby to hurt her. It was the only thing that made sense.

And if breaking her vow of silence meant finding her daughter, she'd reveal her deep, dark secret. Ruby was all that mattered.

"Go on."

"When I arrived at the party, Jerry told me that you'd called and said you weren't coming, that you'd hooked up with another girl. I was hurt," she said in a low voice. "I felt like a fool."

"And Jerry jumped in to console you," he said between gritted teeth. "The son of a bitch."

"He gave me a drink. I'd never had alcohol before," she admitted. "But I was upset so I took a few sips." She pressed her hand to her eyes as the nightmare replayed through her head.

"Leah?"

"Someone…must have slipped something in the drink," she whispered. "I passed out and woke up a while later, but I didn't remember what had happened. Only I was in bed, and I wasn't alone."

"My damn brother slipped a date-rape drug in the drink," Gage said in a brittle tone, "and he raped you?"

She nodded and sucked in another deep breath. She'd gotten this far. She might as well finish.

"There's more," she said, her gut twisting.

He scrubbed a hand over his face. "Jesus."

"After that, I started having nightmares. And I remembered there was someone else there. Another guy. Maybe two. But I couldn't be sure."

He jumped to his feet, pacing back and forth, agitated as if he might hit something. "God almighty, Leah, why didn't you tell someone? Why didn't you go to the police and rat on Jerry? He should have been in jail."

Finally he turned back to her, a dark look in his eyes.

"Why didn't you tell me, Leah?"

"Because I thought you were with another girl," she cried. "I thought you didn't want me." She hugged her arms around her waist, trying desperately to hold herself together. "And I was afraid of him. Afraid you'd hate me and think I was stupid and ugly for letting it happen."

His eyes were stormy. "You didn't let it happen, Leah."

"I know that now. But I was young, and so ashamed and traumatized. I was a virgin, for goodness' sake." She caught her breath. "And then…because I'd been drinking, I thought my parents would blame me. I thought no one would believe me," she said raggedly. "Then Jerry cornered me and warned me if I told anyone he'd do it again. He'd tell everyone I was a slut and that I'd asked for it."

"Bastard."

She had to finish. "And then…"

Another heartbeat of silence stretched between them. "Then what, Leah?" he asked quietly.

She dropped her head forward, her stomach in a knot. "Then I discovered I was pregnant." She finally forced herself to look at him and saw the anger and condemnation as his gaze met hers.

"It killed my father," Leah said. "He had a heart attack two days later. It was my fault."

"No, it wasn't," Gage said heatedly. "The pregnancy is the reason you went away your senior year, isn't it?"

She nodded and swiped at her nose. "Mama thought it would be better for Ruby and me if she raised Ruby as hers. She wanted me to finish school and get a degree so I could make something of myself."

Gage folded his arms, his look lethal. "And you did. Then your mother became ill and you moved back here, and Jerry wasn't happy about it at all. Didn't you think he might have kidnapped Ruby?"

"Yes, but I'd kept my promise. I wanted to protect Ruby. She doesn't know any of this—I never want her to know how she was conceived."

Gage towered over her. Muttering a curse, he stalked to the door. Was he going to give up searching for Ruby?

She wiped at the tears trickling down her cheek. "Where are you going, Gage?"

The fury in his expression sent a chill down her spine.

"I'm going to do what I should have done back then. I'm going to kill my brother."

GAGE SHOOK WITH hatred as he stormed outside.

Leah yelled his name. "No, Gage, don't go. Please."

She caught him at the car, pulling on his arm. "Please don't do anything crazy, Gage. He's not worth it."

He pried her fingers from his arm, his heart pounding, rage eating at his soul. He'd hated the man who'd killed that thirteen-year-old, but he hated Jerry even more. To think that Jerry had bragged about what he'd done, had called Leah a slut when he'd taken her against her will.

Jerry deserved to die. "If he has Ruby, I'll beat it out of him."

"He doesn't know Ruby is mine," she cried. "Please don't tell him, Gage. You can't tell him. I don't want Ruby to know."

That Jerry might be her father. Or one of the other guys… Hell.

"Don't worry, Leah, I won't tell him that. Just how I feel about what a son of a bitch he is." He jumped in the car, slammed the door and tore down the drive, sending gravel spewing.

He'd suspected Leah of hiding something from the beginning, but never had he imagined anything like this. Never had he dreamed that his brother had lied to him about that night, that he'd done something so vile as to rape a girl. And not just any girl—Leah.

The one girl he'd liked and wanted.

That was the reason Jerry had chosen Leah.

Jerry had always hated him and resented him because his parents had given Gage their last name. But he'd never imagined Jerry was vindictive enough to hurt someone because of him.

Guilt made his chest heavy, and he careened around a curve, tires squealing.

So many things made sense now.

Like the fact that Leah didn't drink. She'd said she liked to be in control, because the one time she'd had a drink, she'd paid dearly for it.

She'd also been adamant about not having a boyfriend or lover.

Had she not been with another man since that night?

God...

She'd been a virgin.

Moisture pricked his eyes, but he blinked it away furiously. Her virginity should have been his, dammit, because he'd cared for her. He would have been patient, waiting as long as she wanted. Waiting until she'd loved him.

But Jerry had stolen that from both of them.

Their entire lives might have been different. They might have married. Had a family.

Instead he'd believed his brother, blamed Leah for choosing Jerry and hadn't spoken to her afterward. No wonder she hadn't come to him....

He was an idiot.

Tires screeched as he downshifted around a curve and flew toward the McDermonts' old homestead, a sprawling farmhouse a mile from town. Jerry had stayed on there after the McDermonts had died, then he'd married Dana and they'd made it their family home.

As soon as the white-framed house came into view, Gage's heart picked up its pace. Icicle Christmas lights dangled from the roof edge, green garlands draped the wraparound porch and a homey wreath with a big red bow hung on the front door. The house looked warm and inviting—Dana's doing, probably—but inside the walls lived a monster.

The McDermonts would roll over in their graves if they knew what their son had done.

Night had fallen, shadows from the pines and oaks casting jagged lines on the front lawn and porch. Jerry's fire-engine-red Mustang sat in the driveway, alone, meaning Dana probably wasn't home. Maybe the rumors were true and she'd moved out.

He couldn't blame her. He doubted Jerry had been faithful a day in his life.

Dry, dead leaves rained down as the wind shook them from the trees, and he climbed out and stormed up the porch steps. The winter cold clawed at his face, but it was nothing compared to the ice in his heart.

Hating Jerry with every fiber of his being, he shoved open the door and strode inside. "Jerry, where are you, you lying coward?"

Jerry loped in from the kitchen, a beer in his hand, his hair spiked with gel as if he might be getting ready to go out. "What the hell are you doing here?" Jerry growled.

"You son of a bitch!" Gage pounced on him, jerking him by the collar and shaking him so hard Jerry's eyes bulged with shock.

"What are you doing?" Jerry shouted. "This is my house now, not yours!"

Gage growled in his face. "I'm going to kill you for what you did."

Panic flashed in Jerry's eyes. "Get your damn hands off of me."

"You lying, sniveling bastard!" Gage threw the first punch, his fist connecting with Jerry's jaw. Jerry's head snapped back and he cursed.

"What the hell?"

"I know what you did to Leah, Jerry. You sick lowlife."

"What did that bitch tell you? Whatever she said, it's a damn lie," Jerry insisted.

"The only liar around here is you. You raped her, and then you threatened her into silence. You should be in jail." He threw another punch.

Jerry cursed, blood gushing from his nostrils. "Stop it, you jerk. She's lying, I swear. She asked for it that night. I only gave her what she wanted."

"You are not fit to be on the same planet with Leah Holden, much less in the same room." Gage pushed his face close to Jerry's, rage hardening his tone. "She never wanted you. She wanted me and you couldn't stand it, couldn't stand for me to be happy, so you lied to her and me to keep us apart. Then you drugged her and raped her."

"So what if I did?" Jerry hissed. "You're just a bastard kid that nobody wanted. Somebody had to take you down a notch." Jerry tried to escape, but Gage jerked him back. "You want to know the truth, Gage? Then let me tell you," Jerry said with an evil leer in his eyes. "You missed one fine piece. All the guys had fun that night."

Gage saw red.

He punched Jerry again, so hard he doubled over.

Jerry fought back, but Gage was bigger and stronger. Gage punched him in the gut. Jerry doubled over again but he swung a fist up, connecting with Gage's cheekbone.

Gage cursed, and then kicked Jerry in the chest, sending him to the floor with a shout of pain.

"Stop it, you're going to kill me...." Jerry wheezed, gasping for breath.

Gage tasted the sweetness of vengeance. But he knew he'd lost control, and struggled to regain it, fighting the urge to choke the last breath from his brother's lungs, Leah's pleas not to do anything crazy ringing in his head.

Chapter Thirteen

Leah paced back and forth between the den, the kitchen and Ruby's room, her shoulders knotted with tension as time dragged by.

Had Gage found Jerry? What was he doing? Would he really kill him?

Her emotions boomeranged between gratitude and relief that he had gone to defend her when no one ever had, and humiliation and sadness that she'd told him what had happened.

Jerry and the other guys were sleazebags, and she'd been victimized. But she couldn't quite forgive herself for being stupid enough to take that drink. Not that other women didn't take a drink now and then. There was nothing wrong in a social drink.

And if they hadn't drugged her, she wouldn't have passed out and then…the night would have had a different ending.

Of course, then she wouldn't have Ruby. And heaven help her, she loved that child more than life itself.

She didn't want Ruby to know how she'd been conceived. But if—no, when—Ruby came home, Leah wanted her to know that she was her mother. That she loved her and would make up for the past. That she would be there for her no matter what.

Just as she'd started to imagine that Gage might be.

But that couldn't happen now.

She leaned against the counter, watching the empty tire swing sway in the wind, and her chest tightened. Since when had she begun to depend on Gage?

She couldn't allow herself to. She was broken and…didn't know if she could be fixed.

And when Ruby was home safe and sound, he'd go on with his job to find some woman who didn't have hangups and an illegitimate child.

A child who might belong to his brother, the man she hated. A man who would always remind her of the most painful night of her life.

A man who, in spite of the fact that Gage was furious with him now, was the only family Gage had left.

JERRY COVERED HIS HEAD with his hands and moaned. "I'm gonna call the cops on you!"

"I'll get you the phone!" Gage yelled. "Then we'll have a little party with all those pals of yours and Leah will see that your asses fry."

"She won't do that," Jerry said. "She won't tell. She's too scared."

"She doesn't have to be scared anymore," Gage barked. "I'm here."

"She can't send me to jail," Jerry argued.

"Sure she can. And she can ruin every one of your lives just by revealing the truth. Just think—it will rock Sanctuary to know their golden boys aren't the perfect citizens they thought."

Gage wiped at the sweat pouring down his face and came away with blood.

"But we were just stupid teenagers back then," Jerry said in a pleading tone as he tried to prop himself up against the wall. His shoulder was sagging to one side, and he probably had a few broken ribs.

Gage was still tempted to keep pounding on Jerry, but he reminded himself why he'd been suspended from the force. Anger issues. His temper and his violent side threatened his control.

If he ended up in jail for murder, who would protect Leah? Who would find Ruby?

Charlie Driscill sure as hell couldn't find his ass in a fire and didn't give a crap about Leah or Ruby.

Hell, he hadn't asked Leah for the others' names. He didn't know if he was ready to hear the sickening words.

Jerry leaned precariously to the side, gripping his right arm awkwardly across his chest. His left eye was nearly swollen shut and his lip was bruised and bloody.

Gage needed the truth before Jerry passed out. "Did you kidnap Ruby?"

Jerry moaned and slumped lower against the wall. "Go to hell."

A muscle ticked in Gage's jaw as he grabbed Jerry by the throat. "No, Jerry. That's where you're going. Now, tell me—where is Ruby?"

"I don't know," Jerry whimpered, his bravado dissipating as Gage tightened his hold.

"Don't lie to me. Leah moved back to Sanctuary and that made you nervous, so you took Ruby to scare her, didn't you?"

Jerry shook his head. "No…." he rasped. "I swear, I didn't…."

"Where is she?"

Jerry's left eye was now completely shut, but his right one twitched with panic. "I told you I don't know. I didn't take that stupid kid."

Rage once again exploded through Gage. He wanted to scream that Jerry might be talking about his own child.

But he'd promised Leah.

And he didn't want to give Jerry any claim on Leah or her little girl. He wanted any memory of the bastard erased from her life forever.

"I don't believe you," Gage said.

"I swear on Mama's grave," Jerry gasped.

"Don't you dare," Gage said through a fog of anger.

"Just tell me who kidnapped Ruby. One of the other guys at the party that night?"

"What? She told you there were others?"

Gage's jaw clenched with the restraint it took for him not to beat him to death. "Yes. And I want names."

Jerry shook his head. "No...I told you we've all changed. We've got families, lives now—"

"Leah had a life, but you stole her innocence and destroyed it. And now you're so busy protecting yourself that you're willing to hurt a little girl to keep your dirty secret." He shook him so hard Jerry's teeth rattled. "Give it up, Jerry. Confess what you know."

Jerry gulped. "We were worried," he admitted. "But we warned her and she said she hadn't told anyone."

Gage's heart pounded. "Then what?"

"Someone had heard she'd seen a shrink and so we tapped into the doctor's files. She had told the shrink."

"So you all devised a plan to kidnap Ruby to scare Leah into what? Leaving town?"

"I don't know," Jerry whimpered. "I just tried to intimidate her. I didn't take the kid."

"But you think one of the others did?"

"I don't know for sure. Maybe."

Gage released him with a vicious shove, then reached inside his pocket for his pad and pen. "Write down the name of every guy at that damn party, Jerry. And circle the ones who participated in the rape. If you leave anyone out or I find out you lied, I'll come back and finish what I started. And trust me. Your funeral won't be pretty. I'll bury you in a pine box and make sure everyone in town, including your wife, knows exactly what you are—a vile coward and a rapist."

"I left her when I finished," Jerry said. "I don't know who else was with her." He shoved the pad toward Gage. "But these are the names of the guys at the party."

Jerry scribbled on the pad, and Gage went utterly still as he read the name at the top of the list

The deputy sheriff, Charlie Driscill.

LEAH WANTED TO pull her hair out. Where was Gage? Was he going to come back?

Should she drive over to Jerry's to make sure Gage was all right?

She glanced out the front window and saw Gage's SUV rolling into the drive. Her stomach quivered as he climbed out, the breeze tossing his dark hair across his forehead.

The silhouette of his body in the shadows of the giant oak looked menacing as he strode toward the porch and climbed the steps, and she braced herself to face him.

He rapped on the door three times, and she hurried to let him in. The moment the door opened, a gust of frigid wind slapped her in the face. Then she noticed the cut on his cheek and the bloodstains on his knuckles.

"You're hurt," she whispered, reaching up to touch his cheek. "Let me take care of that cut."

"It's nothing." He gave her a quick, hard glance, then

brushed past her. She closed the door. The fact that he couldn't look at her hurt. "Gage? What happened?"

"He's still breathing."

She crossed her arms, rubbing them with her hands. "I'm sorry, Gage. I didn't want to come between you and Jerry. I… That's one reason I didn't want you to know."

"You didn't come between us. Jerry took care of that the moment he touched you." His voice was heavy, filled with bitterness and anger. "He always hated me. I just never realized how much."

"You mean you don't blame me?" she whispered.

"Dammit, Leah, of course not." He dropped his head forward with a pained groan. "I blame Jerry for being a sick son of a bitch. And I blame myself for not figuring out what he was up to that night, for believing him." He fisted his hands and paced like a wild animal.

"He hurt you to get back at me. He never considered me his brother."

He finally met her gaze, pain glittering in his eyes. "I'll never call him my brother again."

"I'm sorry, Gage, really."

His gaze shot to hers, turmoil hardening his eyes. "Don't apologize again, Leah. It wasn't your fault." He removed a notepad from his pocket and shoved it toward her.

"Look at these names. Jerry said they were the guys at the party. Tell me what you remember. *Who* you remember."

Her hand trembled as she took the notepad, bile rising in her throat as she studied the names. Charlie Driscill. Harry Wiggins. Evan Rutherford. And Jameson Mansfield.

She dropped onto the sofa, and massaged her temples as she tried to sort through her broken memories.

She'd been disappointed, hurt, when Jerry told her that Gage wasn't coming. A bunch of teenagers—the football team and cheerleaders, and some of the other athletes, soccer and baseball players—had gathered out by the pool, laughing and talking. Loud music pulsed through oversize speakers and couples danced on the pool deck, a group of girls in bikinis showing off on the diving board. Two couples lay entwined, making out in lounge chairs, while the guys in the pool chased the girls, trying to untie their tops.

A cooler of beer along with a big tub filled with rum punch sat on the patio. Jerry had offered her a paper cup full of punch, and she'd taken a small sip. It was sweet and smooth, and she'd taken another sip.

A few minutes later, she'd become dizzy.

"Leah?" Gage said.

"I got dizzy," she whispered. "I remember the world spinning, and Jerry came over, laughing. He helped me inside and up the steps to lie down."

"You were at Rutherfords' house?"

She nodded. "His parents were out of town. I collapsed and…" She shook her head and closed her eyes. "Then I woke up and…he was there."

Gage's jaw clenched. "Who else? Driscill?"

A blur of faces paraded in front of her. She remembered Jerry climbing off her and then Charlie had leaned over her and touched her hair. Kissed her. She was crying and tried to push him away, but her body wouldn't function.

Then he took down his pants.

"Yes." She leaned over, breathing in and out deeply, nausea clawing at her. Suddenly she felt Gage sitting beside her.

"I'm sorry, Leah, so sorry." He fisted and unfisted his hands as if trying to maintain control. "So Charlie had his own reasons for not wanting you here. For all we know, he's been covering for himself or the kidnapper."

"I confronted him when Ruby first went missing," she said. "But he assured me that none of them wanted to dredge up the past. He even apologized and said they were sorry for that night, that they'd grown up now." She hesitated. "And since I'd kept quiet, there was no reason for them to do something so drastic. So I assumed a stranger had kidnapped Ruby."

He sucked in a breath. "Who else besides Charlie?"

She pressed her hand against her mouth, swallowing hard to keep from falling apart. "I'm not sure. There was one more face but it's a blur."

He cursed.

"Mansfield, Rutherford and Wiggins were at the party?"

"Yes," she whispered. "But Harry wasn't like them. I don't even know why he was there. He wasn't in their crowd."

"I'm going to call all of them to a meeting tonight,"

Gage said. "If one of them abducted Ruby, we'll push him until he breaks."

He crossed the room and took out his cell.

Leah inhaled a deep breath, working to regain her composure. She was going with him. It was time she stopped running scared and took charge of her life.

Those guys might have gotten away with what they'd done to her eight years ago.

But if they'd kidnapped her daughter, she'd make sure that every single one of them paid.

RUBY WAS STARTING to hate the dark. She'd never been afraid of it before, but sunset marked another day that she hadn't gotten to go home.

Why was this mean man keeping her here?

She'd heard about bad men who did creepy things to little girls, and the first two days she'd been terrified that he'd try to touch her. But he hadn't.

Footsteps pounded up the stairs, and she held her breath, curling her palm around the nail she'd finally freed from the floor. She'd gotten splinters in her fingers and her fingernails were all torn up, but she didn't care. The door screeched open, and she pressed herself against the wall on the cot, hugging her knees to her chest.

His beady eyes glimmered through the holes of the ski mask as he stalked toward her. "It's time to go, kid."

His harsh, cold voice made her shiver. "Where are you taking me?"

"Just shut up and come on." He grabbed her arm and jerked her off the cot.

"I wanna go home. Are you taking me back to Leah?"

A gruff laugh rent the air. "Yeah, kid. Then I'm going to put both of you in the ground."

No! She couldn't let him kill Leah!

She dug her heels in and swung her fists at his sides. He cursed, then bent over to drag her. "Stop fighting me, you stupid kid!"

She gripped the nail between her fingers and jabbed it upward toward his eye, but she connected with his cheek. He shouted an ugly word and slapped her so hard she flew backward against the floor and dropped the nail. She scrambled to find it, but he clawed at her leg.

He slapped her across the face again, then pressed her facedown on the floor and pressed his knee into her back.

"I hate you!" she screamed. "I hate you!"

He ignored her as he tied her hands and ankles. Then he flipped her over, stuffed that stinky rag against her mouth and nose again, and her head began to swim.

A second later she fell into the darkness.

Chapter Fourteen

Gage phoned Charlie and gave him an hour to get Rutherford, Mansfield and Wiggins and meet him at Jerry's. He wanted them to see exactly what he'd done to Jerry.

One of them had to have Ruby. That was the only explanation.

And that meant she was probably still alive. That some stranger passing through hadn't absconded with her.

"I'll be back," he said to Leah. "Try to get some rest."

"No, I'm going with you."

He hesitated. "Leah, I don't think that's a good idea."

She squared her shoulders. "I refuse to let them intimidate me anymore," she said. "I want to face them and make them look me in the eye and tell me the truth."

Admiration for her filled his chest, although he was still hesitant. When she saw Jerry, she'd see just how violent he could get. But he knew she needed to do this. "All right. But be prepared. It'll probably be rough."

"I can handle it," she said. "What I can't handle is not getting Ruby back."

An hour later, Gage parked at Jerry's, then stowed his gun inside his shoulder holster beneath his jacket and they climbed out. Charlie's police cruiser was already there. Gage hissed a breath, preparing himself as they walked up the drive to the porch steps.

"Are you sure you want to do this?" he asked.

She nodded, and he knocked, then pushed open the door. Charlie stood in the foyer wearing his deputy uniform, his gray eyes cold and hard, his hand sliding to his weapon. "You got a lot of nerve calling us all here after what you did to your brother. I ought to lock up your sorry ass for assault."

Gage gritted his teeth. "You and your buddies are the ones who should be in jail, Driscill." He poked at Charlie's badge. "You don't deserve to wear this and you certainly don't deserve to run for sheriff."

Gage leaned closer, meeting Charlie's steely look with one of his own. "I should kill you for what you did to Leah."

"She—"

"Was raped by a bunch of morons," Gage said. "And you damn well know it. And if any of you kidnapped Ruby Holden, I'll make sure that you go to jail and stay there."

He placed his hand on Leah's back and guided her past Charlie to the den where he found Jerry with an icepack on his left eye and a scotch in his hand. Evan and Jameson both stood by the fireplace, their own highball glasses filled to the brim. Evan had been the star quarterback and was the football coach at the high school now. He gave Gage a wary look and avoided looking at Leah as they entered.

Jameson was a lawyer. He had beefed up, his hair loss noticeable, his expression unreadable, his pious attitude in place. Just because his daddy had money, Jameson had always thought he could buy his way out of anything.

Harry Wiggins, the town pharmacist, was still lean with clipped hair, although he wore designer wire-rimmed glasses now instead of the Coke-bottle ones he'd had in high school. He sat in one of the navy wing chairs, his legs jerking in a nervous gesture as he sipped on a beer. He was the odd one, Gage thought. He'd been Leah's friend up until that night.

Had his silence over what had happened earned him a spot with the in-crowd eight years ago?

"I can't believe you came back here," Jerry muttered. "And with *her*."

Gage leaned over and shoved his face into Jerry's. "Unless you're going to tell us who abducted Ruby and where she is, you'd better keep your damn mouth shut."

Charlie's boots pounded on the hardwood floor as he strode in, his arms crossed, his look menacing.

"All right, gentlemen," Gage said. "This has gone on long enough. Your dirty little secret from eight years ago is out. Now, who's going to talk?"

Jameson spoke first. "Whatever you think happened, Gage, is wrong. She has emotional problems and is manipulating you with her lies and false accusations."

Leah jutted out her chin. "You guys drugged me and took advantage of me that night."

Jameson sipped his drink calmly. "You have no proof, nor can you get any." His thick brows bunched with his scowl. "And if you decide to spread such lies, I'll file defamation of character suits that will ruin you financially."

Gage was tempted to pull his gun, but Charlie was armed and dangerous, and he shouldn't take chances with Leah in the room.

"That sounds suspiciously like a threat," Gage said, barely controlling his rage.

"Listen, we were all stupid back then," Evan said quietly. "We did dumb things as kids, everybody did." He waved a chunky hand around the room toward the others. "We all regret that night. At least I know I do." He finally looked at Leah, his expression somber. "And we've tried to make amends by making something of ourselves. That's one reason I chose to teach and coach. To make a difference."

"You shouldn't be allowed to work with young boys," Gage said, sickened at the thought of the chauvinistic, macho attitude the man might pass on.

Evan's jaw tightened, but he bit back a retaliatory comment.

"We don't want trouble," Harry said in a high-pitched tone. He turned to Leah. "I'm sorry for what happened, but we all have lives now and just want to live in peace."

"Peace?" Leah shot back. "You selfish jerks. I was traumatized by what you did. And then I had to come back here to raise my sister, and what do you do? You're so worried about protecting yourselves that you intimidate me. What about my right to live a peaceful life?"

Gage wanted to reach for her, but he didn't dare. Even if these guys hadn't kidnapped Ruby, she deserved this moment to vent her anger and bitterness.

And these men deserved to face her wrath—and the consequences if she decided to go public.

LEAH WANTED TO lash out and hit them all. But the realization that they were terrified of her bolstered her courage.

And knowing Gage was standing up for her gave her strength.

Gage cleared his throat. "Which one of you is responsible for abducting Ruby?"

Jerry shot a nervous look at the others, and Charlie spoke up. "Listen here, you have no reason to accuse anyone in this room of kidnapping." He angled his head toward Leah. "I know you're worried about your sister, and I've done everything I can to help you find her. But you're way off here, Leah."

Leah saw Harry shift nervously. Jameson gave her a haughty look. Evan seemed almost sympathetic.

Gage started to speak, but Leah caught his arm. "I know you guys think I'm vindictive, but I'm not. I don't want to dredge up the past any more than you do, not with my sister around." She sucked in a sharp breath. "All I want is to have her back. She's just a little girl. She doesn't deserve this...." Her voice broke, tears spilling down her cheeks. "Please, if you have her, send her back to me."

"I can't imagine what you're going through," Evan said in a gruff tone. "I have a baby girl, Leah. If I knew where Ruby was, believe me, I'd tell you. But I didn't have anything to do with her kidnapping."

"None of us did," Jameson said defensively.

"Certainly not," Harry murmured. "No way I'd hurt a kid. My wife and I have a little boy of our own."

Leah's hope slid into a downward spiral. She'd been sure one of them had abducted Ruby. Was she wrong?

Harry and Evan both had wives and children. Wouldn't someone in town have seen something suspicious if one of these men had kidnapped a child?

"Day after tomorrow is Christmas Eve," she said in a shaky voice. "Ruby's supposed to sing in the Christmas musical at church. Her angel costume is waiting for her. Her Christmas presents are wrapped and under the tree." She swiped at her tears, hating to beg, but she'd trade her pride—and her life—for Ruby's. "Please. If any of you know where she is, just get her back to me so she can go to the play, so she can wake up in her own bed Christmas morning and find her gifts. No questions asked."

Harry stared at his polished shoes, Jerry at his bruised hands, Jameson into his drink, Evan at the floor. Only Charlie looked her directly in the eye, but he said nothing. Just held her gaze in defiance as if he'd already answered her and had nothing else to say.

"If you got Ruby back, you wouldn't talk?" Jameson asked.

Leah gave him a blistering look. "That's up to you guys. If you have Ruby and I get her back safely, then we'll work something out. If she's hurt or not returned, and I find out one of you took her, I'll make your life a living hell."

She walked over and stared Jameson in the eye. "Understand this," Leah said sharply. "It won't matter to me what kind of false claims or how many suits you file against me, or what you do to me financially. Without Ruby, I don't care, not about money or what the town thinks of me."

Leaving them with that message, she turned and stormed through the room and out the door. Her chest was aching, her stomach knotting into a ball, the room spinning sickeningly with the memory of that painful night.

She stumbled outside, gripping the porch rail, her legs wobbling as she ran down the steps and leaned against a pine, gasping for a breath of clean air and a reprieve from the choking fear consuming her.

GAGE STUDIED EACH of the men in the room. Evan seemed the most sincere. Harry looked terrified, Jameson smug and Jerry ambivalent. Charlie was angry that Leah had dared to accuse them of a crime.

Ironic that Sanctuary was supposed to be a nice, sleepy little town. Magnolia Manor was a haven for children in need and the town had organized a community center for teens and offered support for single mothers. A state-of-the-art women's medical pavilion and fertility center had been built here.

And yet, behind closed doors, some of the residents kept vile secrets.

Had they kidnapped Ruby to keep them hidden?

He still didn't know.

But if one or all of them were guilty, maybe confronting them would force someone to break.

"You want to prove your innocence, then submit fingerprints," Gage said.

"You have no right to ask that," Jameson said.

"I'll do it," Evan said.

Charlie gave him a wary look. "Mine are in the system already."

Harry jerked his leg and glanced at Jameson. "What should we do?"

"If it will clear us," Jameson said, "then let's get it over with."

"You have a kit in your car?" Gage asked Charlie.

Charlie nodded. A few minutes later, each man had been printed. "I'll send them to the crime lab," Charlie said.

"No." Gage didn't trust him. "I'm sending these to a private lab." He headed to the door. "You have until tomorrow," Gage said. "And if Ruby isn't home, I'm calling the feds. Leah may have said no questions asked, but the feds won't be so lenient."

Charlie's mouth tightened, and the others exchanged wary looks. Jerry glared at him with hate.

Why he'd never realized how much he'd detested Jerry, he didn't know.

Because he'd been lost as a kid after his mother had given him away. He had wanted to fit in so badly and please his new family, had craved love so desperately, that he'd worn blinders as to how selfish and spoiled Jerry was.

Leah had said no questions asked.

But he wanted these men to pay for raping her. And if they'd kidnapped Ruby or hurt her, he'd see that they went to jail for a long damn time.

"Ruby deserves to sing at church with her sister. She deserves to wake up and find Santa's gifts." He hardened his voice. "It's two days until Christmas. If you're really sorry about the past and want to make amends, see that she's home tomorrow."

Chest heaving, he stalked outside. Leah was leaning against a tree, pale and shaken. God, he wanted to erase her fear and pain.

She spotted him, and visibly pulled herself together. Affection and concern for her welled in his chest. The girl he'd once known and liked had turned out to be the strongest woman he'd ever met.

And he was falling in love with her.

But would she always see a reminder of the worst night of her life when she looked at him?

He descended the steps, and placed a hand at the small of her back. "I got fingerprints from all of them. Let's drop them at the lab, then I'll take you home."

She nodded and they lapsed into silence while he drove to the lab. He dropped the prints off and explained the circumstances, and the technician agreed to run them quickly. Then he would compare them to the print they'd found on the pie tin.

"What do you think?" she asked as he returned to the Explorer.

"Those bastards are scared and nervous. Maybe one of them will crack."

She pressed her hand to her head and closed her eyes.

He took her other hand and held it as he drove back to her house. When they arrived, he helped her out of the car. She looked so drained and vulnerable, he wanted to wrap her in his arms and never let her go.

But when they reached the door, his heart stalled in his chest. A little doll lay on the porch, dirty and ragged, with blood streaked on its face.

Leah gasped. "Oh my god, it's Ruby's Matilda doll."

Gage's blood ran cold as he spotted the note pinned to the doll's dress.

I WARNED YOU. NOW IT'S TOO LATE.

Chapter Fifteen

Leah knelt and reached for the doll, panic rippling through her.

"Don't touch it, Leah," Gage said. "We might get some DNA from it."

"The note says it's too late," she cried. "What's he done to my baby?"

"I don't know. But don't let your mind go to that dark place, Leah. He's probably just trying to scare you."

A shudder coursed through her as Gage took her keys, unlocked the door and returned a moment later with a bag for the doll. "I'll send this to the crime lab for analysis."

"What good will that do?" she cried. "He said it's too late."

"Don't give up, Leah. He wants to torment you."

She swallowed back a lump of terror and watched numbly as he put Matilda in the bag. Then he brought her inside to sit on the sofa while he punched in the federal agent's number. Her chest ached as he explained her story and relayed their earlier confrontation with Jerry and the other men. When he hung up, his dark gaze met hers, concern in his eyes.

Self-recriminations ate at her. She couldn't believe this was happening. She'd kept that damn vow of silence.

So why had they kidnapped Ruby?

She was trembling, so cold she knew she'd never be warm again. Gage eased down beside her and rubbed her arms. "Go take a hot bath. I'll make you some tea or coffee."

She shook her head. "My stomach can't handle it. I'm losing my mind, Gage. What if he k…illed her?"

"Shh. Don't go there, Leah. We're close to getting her back. I can feel it."

He led her to her bedroom, then coaxed her to lie down and removed her shoes. He stretched out beside her, pulling her into his arms and soothing her with soft whispered words.

"She's coming home," he said. "You can't give up, Leah."

Desperate for comfort, she curled up next to him, inhaling his strength and warmth, then closed her eyes and tried to think positive thoughts.

She imagined Ruby running in on Christmas morning, squealing as she chased the kitten across the floor.

They'd cook pancakes for breakfast, make faces with strawberries and raisins on top and talk about names for the kitten while they ate. Then they'd open presents, and she'd lounge in front of the fire while Ruby drew on the easel with her new markers.

And in her dreams, Gage was there. Watching them, playing with Ruby. Holding Leah's hand. Occasionally they'd sneak a kiss and when Ruby finally went to bed, exhausted and happy, she and Gage would make love.

A sense of peace washed over her, the need to be closer to Gage making her place a hand on his chest. His broad shoulders were sculpted and muscled, his breathing steady and strong. He stroked her hair, then dropped a kiss on her forehead. Outside, the wind howled, cold air seeping through the eaves, and a branch scraped the window.

They lay there for a long time in the dark, the tension between them mounting as her desire for him grew. He hadn't asked her for anything, had been nothing but a gentleman, had stood up for her and protected her when she thought she was all alone.

She didn't want to be alone. Not anymore.

And she didn't want to feel this unbearable pain and fear that consumed her.

Years ago, Jerry had overpowered her, and the others had either participated or watched. She wanted to regain her power now. She refused to let Jerry ruin her future, or her chances to be normal and to have the love of a good man.

And Gage was that. He'd proven it over and over again.

Summoning her courage, she slid a hand up and cupped his jaw, then kissed him. His breath caught in surprise, but he pressed her closer, then claimed her mouth with his. His lips were gentle, yet she felt his need as he slipped his tongue inside her mouth and deepened the kiss. Fire blazed in her belly, his touch eliciting erotic sensations so foreign that she craved more.

He pressed her closer, his body hard against hers, pulsing with need, stirring her hunger to a frenzy.

She wanted more. Wanted to touch him and to be touched, to drive away the fear and know that she was alive.

To make love to him and forget that she'd ever known the violence of rape. To know that he would still be in her life once Ruby came home.

That she'd have her daughter and a man to love, just as she'd always wanted.

GAGE SAVORED Leah's taste, his body humming with arousal, the need to be with her—to love her and erase the past—stronger than anything he'd ever felt in his life.

But he had to take things slowly.

He tried to banish the image of Jerry's or any other man's hands on her against her will, and show her the pleasure he wanted to give her. The pleasure she deserved.

And a reprieve from the pain and worry she'd endured the past few days. Hell, the past few years.

He held her, inhaling her scent as he traced his tongue along the edge of her lips, sipping at her mouth, savoring her sweet goodness and warmth.

Leah was the marrying kind of girl. The kind a man would want to keep and treasure. The girl he'd wanted years ago. The woman he admired and wanted now.

She sighed, quivering beneath his touch, and trailed her hand over his chest, purring as he flicked his tongue along her neck. His own body sizzled with hunger, fire stirring in his loins.

She clung to him as he lowered his head and dropped teasing kisses along her neck and her breasts. She moaned as he teased her nipples beneath her blouse. He reached for the top button, then paused and looked into her eyes.

"Leah?"

"Yes," she whispered. Even in the dark room, he could see her eyes were glazed with passion, her lips parted, her cheeks flushed with heat. Raw hunger flared inside him, spiking his own need to a frenzied heat.

"Tell me if you want me to stop."

"I don't," she said on a raspy breath. "Please, Gage, I want you. I always did."

Her softly spoken admission tripped every nerve ending in his body, every unleashed desire, every ounce of the yearning he'd had for her years ago and still carried now.

"I want you, too," he murmured. "But I don't want to hurt you."

She kissed him, arching her body into his. "You won't. I know you won't."

Adrenaline, fear, raw, primal passion exploded in his

chest. He slowly unbuttoned her blouse, teasing her skin with his tongue as he opened her top to reveal a pair of perfect breasts covered in pink lace. They were full and ripe, spilling over the edges of the lace, her nipples taut peaks begging for his mouth.

All control vanished. He unfastened the front clasp, her heavy breasts spilling out, and he teased her right nipple with his fingers while he bent over the other, drawing the turgid peak into his mouth.

She moaned and cried out, her body trembling beneath him. His length hardened and throbbed, aching to be inside her, his need all consuming. But he ordered himself to slow down, to make sure Leah wanted him. He'd do anything for Leah.

Including walk away if she asked him to.

A sharp pang splintered his chest. No, it wouldn't come to that.

Although how could it not?

He shut out the voice of fear inside his head, and traced his fingers over her shoulder.

Sucking her nipple deeper into his mouth, he fed like a starving man. Then he offered her other breast the same loving attention. She groaned his name, threading her fingers through his hair, and he lowered one hand to trace her spine, her hips and to rub against her heat.

Her hips arched to meet his, hunger and need in her touch as she coaxed him to her, and he reached for her zipper, desperate to feel her bare skin beneath his fingers, her flesh quivering against his, her orgasm tremoring through her body as he claimed her.

But just as he began to slide off her jeans, a loud gust of wind jarred the air around him and glass shattered.

He threw his body over hers, shielding her as a fire-lit torch soared through the room and dropped onto the floor, exploding into flames below the window.

LEAH SCREAMED AS Gage covered her with his body, pressing her into the mattress.

Smoke billowed up, the curtains catching on fire. Gage jumped off the bed, pulling her with him, grabbed the spread and began to try to douse the flames. "Call the fire department, then get out!" Gage shouted.

She hastily rebuttoned her blouse as she ran to the den for the phone. Panic caught in her throat, but she swallowed it back and dialed the fire department. Then she hurried to the laundry room, retrieved the fire extinguisher and took it to Gage. The fire had spread to the braided rug, and she coughed as smoke filled her lungs.

"I'll try to contain the blaze," Gage said. "Go outside, Leah."

She ran back to the den and looked at the tree and the gifts.

She had to save the pictures and Ruby's presents.

Frantic, she grabbed the photo album her mother had put together chronicling Ruby's childhood as well as her mother's photo from the fireplace mantel, and ran outside, tossing them onto the grass. Then she went back inside, gathered Ruby's gifts in her arms and carried them outside.

Remembering Ruby's favorite blanket, her treasure chest of memories and her favorite bear, Leah raced into her room to rescue them.

Outside, the blare of the fire engine rent the night and she took Ruby's things to the porch just as it screeched up her drive. Three firemen jumped down from the truck and raced toward her.

"Where did it start, ma'am?"

"My bedroom. Gage McDermont is trying to contain it with a fire extinguisher."

"Stay back," the other man ordered.

She nodded and ran down the steps to stand by the big oak tree. Her heart raced and she prayed she wouldn't lose the house—not the home she'd grown up in, Ruby's home.

A twig snapped behind her and someone grabbed her from behind, holding a rag over her face. She choked, fighting and trying to scream, but her legs went limp.

Then the world swam in a drunken rush, and darkness overcame her.

THE LAST EMBERS DIED as the firefighters rushed in, but smoke filled the room in a cloud of white and the scent of charred fabric clogged the air. "It's out," Gage told the firemen.

"What happened?" one of them asked.

"Someone threw a torch through that window."

The firefighters both glanced at the broken window and charred curtains. "You mean arson?"

Gage nodded. "That and attempted murder. Will you have a crime unit and arson investigator process this room?"

They nodded and Gage hurried outside to tell Leah that the blaze was out and there had been minimal damage. Coughing from the smoke, he inhaled the fresh air to steady his breathing. Christmas presents lay scattered on the grass by the front porch, and he stepped over a small chest and several pictures, scanning the yard for Leah.

Where in the hell had she gone?

He glanced at the carport and the car, but didn't see her. His lungs tightened, and a knot of fear settled in his stomach.

"Leah?" He checked the fire truck but it was empty. Panicked, he turned in a wide arc, shouting her name and searching the yard. Leah was nowhere in sight.

Fear clawed at him as he spotted a section of grass that had been flattened and crushed, the leaves scattered as if someone had been dragged toward the woods.

Whoever had set the fire had waited around to see if it killed them.

And he'd abducted Leah while Gage was inside trying to extinguish the flames.

THE MEAN MAN said he was going to kill her sister.

Ruby had to find a way to stop him.

Tears leaked from her eyes, but she couldn't wipe them away because her hands were still tied behind her back. She rolled over on her side, searching the darkness to figure out where she was.

The floor was icy cold and hard. The place smelled old and musty, and she thought she heard something skittering across the floor.

A mouse or a rat?

She wiggled up to a sitting position, feeling around on the floor behind her to find something to untie her hands. If she only had that nail…but she'd lost it.

She choked back a sob, and made herself inch along the floor, searching, but the room was tiny and cramped, like a closet. Something creepy crawled across her leg, and she screamed, jerking her foot back and forth to shake it off.

The door screeched open, and she pulled back as far as she could, shaking all over. He'd come to kill her!

She thought he was going to reach for her, but instead, he shoved something inside. It fell onto the floor with a clunk.

She sucked in a breath, and leaned over in the dark to see what it was. Oh, no…

It was a body.

Her hands shook as she tried to see the face.

Leah!

She doubled over, sobbing. Leah wasn't moving.

Chapter Sixteen

Leah stirred, her head throbbing, a strange, bitter taste in her mouth. Blinking to focus in the dark, she scrambled to figure out where she was. A small closet somewhere. But where?

From the corner, soft cries wrenched the air.

She turned her head and saw a small huddled shadow, sobbing into her knees.

Ruby?

She tried to call out, but her throat was so dry it felt as if her mouth had cotton in it. "Ruby?" Thank God, it was her—she was alive. "Ruby, baby, it's all right."

Slowly Ruby raised her head and looked at her, her little body shaking. "Leah?"

"Yes, honey, I'm here now. Don't cry."

Ruby lunged forward, her movements awkward with her feet bound together and her hands tied behind her back. Anger churned through Leah at the sight. Her hands and feet were bound, as well, but she struggled to sit up. She had to get to Ruby, hug her, console her, find a way to escape.

When Ruby made it to her, she fell against Leah's chest, her body trembling with sobs.

"I was so scared, Leah. I thought he k…illed you."

"No, I'm okay. How about you?" She craned her neck, searching for injuries, but it was so dark she could hardly see Ruby's small face. "Did he hurt you, Ruby?"

"N…o," she cried. "But I don't like him. He's mean. He said you didn't want me anymore."

"Oh, no, Ruby. I love you. I've been out of my mind with worry looking for you. I called the police and the FBI and I have a private investigator now hunting for you."

"I wanna go home."

Leah fought with the bindings around her wrists, aching to take Ruby into her arms, to promise her she'd save her and take her home, that she'd never let anyone hurt her again.

"I know, honey. And I'll find a way to get us out of here. I promise." She pushed up to a sitting position, but the room swayed, and she had to close her eyes to keep from passing out again. When she opened them, Ruby leaned against her as if she desperately needed to know that Leah was really there, that she wasn't dying.

Her poor little girl. She wanted to kill whoever had done this to her.

"Have you been here the entire time?" Leah asked.

Ruby shook her head. "N…o." She rubbed her runny

nose on her sleeve. "First I was in an old house, in an attic room." She gulped for a breath, sniffling. "But last night he came in and put a rag over my mouth." She sniffed again. "I don't remember how we got here."

He'd chloroformed Ruby, too.

"I tried to run away," Ruby whispered. "I scratched him with a nail, and he got mad and slapped me."

Leah fought to control her fury.

"Do you know who he is?"

"No."

"Have you seen his face?" Leah asked. "Can you tell me what he looks like?"

She shook her head. "He's tall and mean and wears a ski mask," she said, fear lacing her voice. "And he's got stubby fingers."

Leah had to think. "We have to untie these ropes," she said. "I want you to scoot so your back is against mine, and I'll untie you, then you can untie me. Okay?"

Ruby nodded. "Leah, we have to hurry. He's going to kill us."

GAGE WAS GOING out of his mind.

He drove to the police station to find Driscill. Deputy Rainwater was there, and Gage explained about the fire and that Leah was missing.

"Where's Driscill?" Gage asked.

Rainwater scowled. "You think Driscill had something to do with the kidnapping?"

"If he didn't kidnap them, he may know who did," Gage said.

The deputy dropped his boots from the desktop with a thud. "He's probably at home."

"Get the other deputy and round up Jerry, Jameson Mansfield, Evan Rutherford and Harry Wiggins, and bring them in for questioning."

Confusion colored the deputy's eyes. "What's going on?"

"I can't explain now, but these men are connected and may be involved in both kidnappings."

Rainwater considered Gage for a moment, and then he stood, adjusting his weapon in his holster. "I'll call Cramer and we'll get right on it."

"I'm going to find Driscill."

Gage hurried outside, battling a blustery wind. He jumped in his SUV and drove toward Driscill's on the outskirts of town. He lived on a secluded dirt road in a cabin overlooking one of the ridges. As Gage parked and climbed out, storm clouds rumbled above, the gray sky ominous, and a few snowflakes fluttered to the ground.

He checked his gun inside his jacket, prepared to use it if needed. More snowflakes rained down, glittering on the grass as he climbed the stoop. Angry voices sounded inside.

"Dammit, son, what have you done now?"

It was Charlie's father, Billy. Gage paused and listened for Charlie's reply.

"Nothing, Dad, but Gage McDermont is dangerous.

He threatened to expose us all for what happened eight years ago."

"You stupid son of a bitch!" Billy shouted. "I knew when that Holden girl came back, there'd be trouble."

"She promised not to tell," Charlie said.

Billy broke into a coughing attack. "But she did tell, didn't she?"

"Yes," Charlie snarled. "First that shrink, then Gage. And he won't leave it alone."

"I've fixed your messes all your life, but if this comes out, and people learn I covered it up, then it's on my head, too." Billy wheezed a breath, sounding disgusted. "I worked too hard running this town to have the locals turn on me in my golden years."

"No one has to know you covered up anything," Charlie argued. "But if it comes out, then my life—my future as sheriff—is over."

There was a long, tense pause. "Am I going to have to fix this, or are you going to do it yourself?" Billy asked.

Gage eased open the door and inched inside. Billy was pacing the wood floor, his hair and clothing disheveled, a cigarette dangling from his mouth. Charlie sat slumped forward in a chair, his head in his hands.

"Just how are you suggesting he fix the problem?" Gage asked.

Charlie and Billy jerked their heads up in unpleasant surprise. "What in the hell are you doing here?" Charlie growled.

"I came to find out if you tried to burn down Leah's house, and if you kidnapped her," Gage said sharply. "Where is she, Driscill?"

"Get out," Billy said. "You've got no right coming in our house and accusing my son of something illegal."

"He raped an innocent young girl eight years ago," Gage said.

"Which is a nonissue now," Billy said.

"It goes to motive," Gage said. "Now, have you added kidnapping and attempted murder to your list, Charlie?"

Charlie's panicked gaze shot to Gage's. "I didn't kidnap the kid or Leah. And I haven't killed anyone."

"Why should I believe you?" Gage asked.

"Because I didn't do it," Charlie barked. "I confronted Leah when she first returned to town, and I knew she was scared enough not to talk. Why would I have kidnapped the kid when she was keeping her mouth shut?"

"To scare her," Gage said. "Then she called the cops and the feds poked their noses in and things got complicated."

Charlie stood, nose to nose with him, eyes flaring with anger. "You may have the motive right, but you've got the wrong man." He angled his head toward his father. "Believe me, I've tried over the years to atone for that night by serving the law and making my father proud."

Billy shrugged his beefy shoulders. "And now the truth's going to come out anyway."

"Leah had no intention of exposing what happened that

night," Gage said. "She wanted to protect Ruby. So if the truth comes out, blame whoever kidnapped Ruby."

Gage's cell phone rang and he flipped it open. "McDermont."

"It's Deputy Rainwater. I've got Mansfield and Rutherford and we're on our way to the station."

"And Jerry?"

"Cramer's looking for him."

"How about Wiggins?"

"I haven't gone by there yet."

"I'll check on him," Gage said, "then meet you at the station."

"You've got my deputy working for you?" Charlie asked, his eyes hard and cold.

"He wants to solve this case," Gage said. "Unlike you."

A muscle ticked in Charlie's jaw. "I will solve it," Charlie said. "Let's go pick up Wiggins. I know dirt on all of them. I'll push until someone talks."

For the first time since he'd returned, Gage sensed that Charlie might be on his side. On Leah's side.

He only hoped he hadn't misjudged him. Otherwise Charlie was leading him right into a trap.

LEAH TWISTED SIDEWAYS toward Ruby, and Ruby angled her body so they were back to back. Fumbling in the dark, Leah found Ruby's hand and squeezed it.

"I love you, Ruby."

"I love you, too," Ruby whispered. "But I'm scared."

"I know, honey, and you've been so brave. We're going to get out of here, I promise."

"Why did the man take me?" Ruby asked, her voice warbling.

Leah inhaled a calming breath, determined to reassure Ruby. Gage would have figured out she'd been kidnapped by now. He'd be searching for her and wouldn't give up until he found them.

"He wanted to hurt me." She squeezed Ruby's hand one more time, then found the knot and began to untie her hands. "And he knew how much I loved you."

"Why would he want to hurt you?" Ruby whispered.

Leah closed her eyes. Amazingly, some of the trauma from eight years ago had lifted. Maybe by finally telling someone, by allowing herself to trust a man, she was healing.

Maybe she could have a normal life, a lover, maybe even get married and give Ruby a little sister or brother.

One who looked like Gage.

Heaven help her, she was in love with him.

"Leah?"

"Yes, honey. I'm sorry, I was just thinking." She caught the end of one of the loops and wove it back through the knot. "A long time ago, when I was in high school, something happened. A bunch of us had a party that got out of hand and…the guys at the party wanted to keep it quiet."

"What happened?"

"They were drinking," Leah explained as a drop of perspiration trickled down her neck. "And I got hurt. Anyway, they were afraid I'd tell." She gave the rope a final tug. "There, I've got it."

Ruby slipped her hands free of the ropes, and Leah sighed in relief. "Now, can you untie your feet?"

"Yes," Ruby said confidently. She bent over and struggled with the rope, hissing between her teeth as she fought to undo the knots. "I got it!"

"Good. Untie my hands now."

Ruby crawled to Leah and hastily worked on her bindings. Her breathing rattled in the tense quiet, and Leah listened for footfalls or a voice, anything to indicate their abductor had returned.

"I almost got it," Ruby said quietly.

The smell of dirt and chemicals and foliage overwhelmed Leah. She was sweating, and she imagined Ruby was, too. "Good girl, you're doing great, Ruby."

She felt the ropes loosening, a seed of hope stirring inside her. If he returned, she had to stall, to do something to keep them alive until Gage could find them.

"I did it!" Ruby whispered.

Leah shook off the ropes, then leaned over and untied her feet, silently swearing at the heavy knot. It felt like an eternity, but she finally jerked the ropes free, then looked up at Ruby, running her hands over her face and shoulders.

"Are you really all right, honey?"

"Yes."

Her voice sounded tiny, and even in the dark, she could

see Ruby's lower lip quiver. She was trying to be so brave, but she must have been terrified over the last few days.

"Come here." Leah pulled her into her arms and Ruby fell against her, her body trembling, more tears falling.

"I wanna go home and sleep in my own bed," Ruby cried. "I wanna be there for Christmas."

"I know, honey, we will be." Leah prayed she was right. "There's something else I have to tell you."

Ruby sniffled. "What?"

Leah stroked Ruby's hair from her face, drying her tears. "It's about that night, Ruby. That night at the party I told you about."

"Yeah?"

"That night, I got pregnant."

"You had a baby?" Ruby asked. "Where is it?"

Leah swallowed back her emotions, then tilted Ruby's chin up so she could look in her eyes. "I'm holding her in my arms. You're not my sister, Ruby. You're my daughter."

Chapter Seventeen

Gage followed Charlie to Harry Wiggins's house, a small A-frame with an immaculately landscaped yard. It was almost midnight now. Leah had been gone for hours.

He struggled not to let his imagination go wild, but each second that passed lessened the chances that Ruby and Leah would survive.

Whoever had abducted them had panicked now, and a panicked man was dangerous and out of control.

He parked in the drive and followed Charlie up to the door, waiting as Charlie pounded on it. A minute later, a young woman with a toddler on her hip answered.

Her wary gaze flickered over Charlie, then to Gage. "Deputy?"

"Jeanie, I'm here to see Harry. Is he here?"

Her lips thinned, and the baby scrunched his nose and began to fuss so she jiggled him up and down, soothing him. "Guess you haven't heard. Harry doesn't live here any longer."

Charlie leaned against the door. "When did you two split?"

"A few weeks ago. He's been staying in one of his parents' old rental houses in the mountains. What's this about, anyway? Did Harry do something?"

"I need to talk to him," Charlie said in a noncommittal tone. "Do you know which cabin?"

She walked to the sofa table, scribbled an address, then handed it to him. "There's a greenhouse there. Harry's nuts about that place." She glanced at Gage. "What did Harry do? Is he in trouble?"

Gage wanted answers and didn't have time for Charlie to coddle this woman. "It's about Ruby Holden's kidnapping. Her mother, Leah, is missing now, too."

"Oh my gosh." Jeanie hugged her baby closer, and he nestled against her shoulder, eyes drooping. "You think Harry knows something about that kidnapping?"

"You tell us," Gage said. "Has he said anything to you? Been acting strange or secretive lately?"

She worried her bottom lip with her teeth. "Well, a little. I mean, he was always a fanatic about some things, but the last few months he's been really nervous and wired, his behavior kind of erratic. He snapped at me and Will a lot." She rubbed the baby's back, rocking him back and forth. "I asked him what was wrong and he just got mad. He was always up at that greenhouse, too, and said he was going to build a second one. I hate to say it, but he was taking pills, too. OxyContin. I caught him and he turned almost violent. That's when I gave him the choice of cleaning up or getting out."

"And he left?" Gage asked.

She nodded. "He was furious. I told him that unless he proved he was drug free, I was going to get full custody of Will." She shrugged. "I grew up in an abusive home. I sure as heck wasn't going to raise my son in one."

Gage and Charlie exchanged looks. "Thanks, Jeanie," Charlie said.

"I don't understand what that has to do with the Holden girl," she said.

"Harry never mentioned her or Leah?"

She frowned. "Well, I did hear him talking to Jameson Mansfield on the phone one night. And he said her name. It sounded like he didn't like her moving back to town, but he never told me the reason."

"Thanks," Gage said, then glanced at the baby. "We'll let you put your son down now."

She gave him a curious look. "All right. But I hope you find the little girl and Leah."

"We will," Gage said. He only hoped they were still alive when he did.

LEAH STUDIED RUBY, praying she didn't hate her.

"I don't understand," Ruby whispered.

"I know, honey, and I didn't mean to lie to you." She stroked Ruby's tangled hair, aching to be home so she could wash it and brush it for her. "I was just a kid, only sixteen, and Mama thought it would be better for you and for me if she raised you like you were hers. She wanted me to finish school so I could make something of myself, and... I loved you, Ruby. I don't want you to think that I didn't want to be your mother. But I was just so young." Her voice choked.

Ruby burrowed into her arms. "It's okay, Leah," she said softly. "I loved Mama and I miss her, but you can be my mommy now."

Tears trickled down Leah's face. "Oh, yes. I want that. I want that so much."

"I love you. And I knew you'd come for me." Ruby hugged her. Leah was grateful and relieved that the truth was out, that she could finally be free of her dark secrets.

Footsteps suddenly clattered outside, and she and Ruby both tensed. She held Ruby tighter, hating the fear trapping them.

If this man tried to hurt her daughter, she'd kill him— or die trying.

"I'LL PICK UP JERRY and meet you at the station," Charlie said.

Gage hesitated, unsure whether to trust him or not. But Charlie seemed determined to make things right now, so he nodded.

He raced to the station, frantic for answers.

Mansfield gave him a go-to-hell look when he entered, but Evan seemed concerned.

"Deputy Rainwater said someone kidnapped Leah," Evan said.

Gage nodded. "First they tried to burn her house down."

"Good God," Evan said.

Mansfield folded his arms. "You can't possibly think one of us had something to do with this."

"Where were you earlier tonight?" Gage asked.

Evan sighed. "With my wife and child. You can call her and ask. I like to be there to put the baby to bed at night."

Gage glanced at Rainwater. "Will you see if his alibi checks out?"

The deputy nodded, then stepped aside to make the call.

"How about you, Mansfield?"

He cut his gaze sideways. "With a client for dinner," he said. "We didn't break until about a half hour ago."

Gage gestured toward his notepad. "Write down the client's phone number."

Rainwater hung up and confirmed Evan's story.

"I don't have to do what you say," Mansfield said.

Driscill walked in with a belligerent-looking Jerry in tow. Gage took one look at him and knew he was drunk. "Found him at the pub. He's been there for hours." Driscill glanced at Mansfield. "And you're right, you don't have to do what McDermont says. But you do have to answer to me. Write down the name and number of that client."

Jerry slouched down in the chair, his eyes glassy, his breath reeking of beer.

The only person missing was Wiggins. Where was he?

While the deputy called Mansfield's client, Gage phoned the crime lab. "Listen, did you match any of those prints I sent in with that partial from the dog bowl we found at the rental house?"

"Just a minute, and I'll run them."

"Make it fast," Gage said. "Try Harry Wiggins's print first. Leah Holden has been kidnapped, too. We may be running out of time to find her and her daughter."

Gage rapped his knuckles on the desk while he waited, his nerves strung tight as he imagined what Leah and Ruby might be going through.

"You're right," the CSI said. "It's a match."

Gage ground his teeth. So Harry had used a dog to lure Ruby. Had she heard the dog and opened the window? "All right. Thanks."

When he hung up, Rainwater cleared his throat. "Mansfield's alibi checked."

"Wiggins has her," Gage said. "His print matched the one we took at the rental house. And if he's taking Oxy-Contin, his behavior may be erratic, so we have to consider him high, desperate and potentially violent."

Grim looks floated around the room in the tense silence. "I'm going to find him," Gage said. "And if any of you conspired to help him—"

Evan stood. "I'll help search."

Gage shot him a suspicious look, but if any of the men regretted what they'd done as teenagers, it was obviously

Evan. Still, did he trust him enough to let him go with them?

Gage shook his head at Evan, then gestured toward Rainwater. "Stay here with all of them. I don't want to take the chance that one of them will phone Wiggins and warn him we're onto him."

He headed to the door but Driscill came up behind him. "I'll drive. I know this country like the back of my hand."

Gage still didn't like the man, but time was of the essence, so he agreed and they hurried to Driscill's squad car. Driscill sped from the parking lot and drove through the town square, then headed out of town. The mountain roads were dark and desolate, snow heaping on the trees and road. Driscill turned on the defroster and wipers, braking before a curve in the road.

"He was always such a wimp, a total science geek in school," Driscill said.

"He wanted to fit in, to be a part of the popular crowd," Gage said through gritted teeth. "And since he knew your dirty secrets, you guys let him into your tight group."

"Actually, Harry had the drug. In a way, the whole thing was his idea."

The temperature had dropped to below freezing, the wind whistling through the trees in an ominous roar as they drove deeper into the mountains. Charlie turned onto a narrow, paved road leading toward an area called Blindman's Bluff. The trees were thick and dense, the drive steep, the snow blanketing the ground in a sea of white.

Another mile on the winding road and they reached the cabin at the top of the ridge. Although there was no car in sight, Gage hit the ground running, drawing his gun as he approached the dark cabin. The wind beat his face, the chill of winter reminding him that if Leah and Ruby were out in the woods, they might not survive.

Driscill moved up beside him, narrowing his eyes at Gage's weapon but refraining from comment. Gage inched up to the window and peered inside. The cabin was old, the windows dirty, the inside dark and quiet, seemingly empty.

"I'll check inside," Driscill said.

"I'll look around outside and check the storage building."

Gage tugged the collar of his coat up to fight the bitter wind, then dashed to the side to the metal storage building, jiggling the locked door. In spite of the cold, sweat beaded on his skin as he ran to the carport and found a pair of bolt cutters, then hurried back to the storage building to cut the lock.

"Leah?" He peered inside, moving slowly, searching the shadows. Old tools, potting soil, planters, a wheelbarrow and various other gardening supplies filled the inside, but no Leah or Ruby.

He went back to the house and met Driscill at the door. "There's no one inside," Driscill said. "But I did find several pill bottles. It looks like Jeanie was right."

"Any indication that Leah or Ruby had been there?"

Driscill shook his head. "No. Just some dirty dishes and Wiggins's clothes."

Gage peered down the road. "Maybe he took them to the greenhouse."

"Let's check it out. It's about a mile from here."

They hurried back to the car, battling the wind, Gage's pulse pounding. If Wiggins wasn't at the greenhouse where else would he take Leah and Ruby?

Terrifying scenarios raced through his head. He could have killed them and left their bodies in the mountains for the wild animals. Or dropped them over a ridge.

And with the heavy snow falling now, even if they were alive, by the time they found them, they might not survive the elements.

HARRY PAUSED OUTSIDE the storage closet as his cell phone rang, and he stared at the number. His wife.

His breath caught in his throat. Was she calling to say she'd changed her mind? That she wanted him back? That she would let him see his kid anytime he wanted?

That she wouldn't spread rumors about him having a drug problem?

Sweat exploded on his brow beneath the ski mask, and he scrubbed at the material, trying to soak it up as he connected the call.

"Harry, it's Jeanie."

His heart was racing fast, so fast he pressed his hand over it. "What do you want?"

"The sheriff and a man named Gage McDermont were

just here. They think you had something to do with that Holden girl's disappearance. Please tell me that's not true."

Shit. That damn Gage McDermont. He'd known when that guy had come back to town asking questions he'd be trouble. Charlie would have handled things fine, let the girl's kidnapping go unsolved. And eventually, Harry would have returned her to her sister, and let her know that if she didn't keep her stupid mouth shut, the kid would die the next time.

"Harry!" Jeanie screeched. "Answer me. The sheriff said Leah is missing now, too. You didn't do anything to her or her sister, did you?"

He wheezed a breath, feeling an asthma attack coming on. Hell, he hadn't had one in years—not until Leah Holden had decided to move back to Sanctuary.

"What did you tell them, Jeanie?"

A long pause. "The truth. That you have a drug problem."

"Hell, why did you do that? I thought you loved me, Jeanie."

"Harry, did you hurt Leah or her sister? Because if you did, you'll never see your son again."

"Of course I didn't hurt them." Harry leaned over, removing his inhaler from his pocket and breathing in the medicine. He was shaking as he tried to catch a breath.

How had things gotten so screwed up so fast? He'd kept silent all these years because he'd finally found a place in the town. Thanks to Charlie, Evan and Jameson, everyone thought he was okay.

Sanctuary was his town now, dammit. He had friends here, and everyone at the pharmacy loved him.

He disconnected the call.

Leah Holden had ruined everything.

It was time for her to die.

Chapter Eighteen

Leah stood and pushed Ruby behind her as the door opened. She'd taken a self-defense class in college and tried to remember the key points as the masked man filled the doorway. The shiny metal of a gun glinted in the darkness, and she sucked in a breath.

"Who are you?" Leah asked, forcing herself to sound calm for Ruby's sake, and hoping she could reason with her abductor. Gage had to be looking for them—if she could just stall… "Come on, you coward, show your face."

He shook his head and reached for her, the gun aimed at her chest. She had to outsmart him. "Talk to me," she said. "Tell me why you're doing this."

"You know why," he growled. "You promised never to tell."

She strained to identify his voice, but it sounded muffled through the mask.

"And I kept my promise," she said. "So there was no need to kidnap us."

"But you did tell. You told that shrink."

Leah was shocked.

"Jameson found out. He told us all and warned us that you might be trouble."

"My psychiatrist was sworn to secrecy by patient confidentiality," she argued.

"But you had to move back," he continued. "Had to insinuate yourself into this town as if you belonged. But it's been eight years, and I'm not going to let you expose what happened when we were kids."

"I belong in Sanctuary just as much as anyone else," she said, hating the way Ruby was trembling behind her. "It's my home and I won't let you run me off again."

"You should have taken the kid and moved away," he said. "Just seeing you every day reminded us all about that night."

"You should remember because it's haunted me. Maybe it's time you felt some guilt."

"No, I've worked too hard to fit in for you to mess with me now."

"I never planned to expose any of you," she said. "I only wanted to give Ruby a home. Let us go and this will be over."

"It's too late for that," he said, his hand shaking as he waved the gun. "You and the kid have to die."

Leah didn't intend to go down without a fight. The scent of his sweat permeated the air, his breath rancid and labored.

He stepped forward, and she lunged at him, knocking his armed hand upward. A shot rang out, and she screamed for Ruby to run.

"Get out of here, baby!"

Ruby dashed around him just as he dove for Leah. She clawed at his face, tearing at his mask, determined to see the man who'd stolen her daughter. He tried to grab her but she jerked off the mask and shock slammed into her.

Harry.

An image flashed into her head—the guy climbing on her. But this time she saw his face. Not Evan or Jameson, but Harry.

Nausea rose to her throat. Evan and Jameson had only watched, but Harry had participated.

"You," she whispered. "You were my friend. The one I trusted."

"I wanted you but you didn't even notice me." He slid a hypodermic from the pocket, its shiny point glinting in the dark.

"You wanted to be part of their group so bad that you violated me."

"You weren't supposed to remember anything," Harry shouted. He grabbed for her, but she jumped back and kicked the needle from his hand, sending it flying to the corner.

Fury spurned her adrenaline, and she stomped his instep with all her force, raising her leg to knee him in the crotch, but he sidestepped the blow, grabbed her by the throat and jammed the gun to her temple.

She went utterly still. She'd never intended to let any of the men know the truth about Ruby, but if it was the only way to save Ruby's life, she'd do it. "You can't kill Ruby," she said.

His breath bathed her face. "Why not?"

"Because she's my child," Leah whispered.

His hand tightened on her throat, gripping her painfully. "What?"

"That means you might be her father," Leah said. "You couldn't kill your own child, could you, Harry?"

GAGE'S HEART STAMMERED at the sound of gunfire.

Cursing, he took off running. Charlie followed behind him, both drawing their weapons as they hurried through the dense brush. Finally they reached the clearing, the wind blowing snow in a blinding haze around them. Through the blur, he spotted the greenhouse, and saw a small shadow darting around the edge of the building.

An animal?

No, a little girl. Ruby.

Thank God she was alive.

He shoved past a pine tree, and headed straight for her. She paused, searching the woods, then crouched down low by the building and grabbed a stick as if to defend herself. He slowed behind her, not wanting to scare her, but he had to keep her quiet in case Wiggins was out here looking for her.

He signaled to Charlie to indicate what he was doing,

and Charlie motioned that he'd check the building. Gage moved silently, inch by inch until he was behind Ruby, then slid a hand to her mouth.

Ruby swung around, slapping at him with the stick, but he caught her arm and held her in his grip. "Shh, Ruby, my name is Gage. I'm a friend of Leah's."

She scratched at him, clawing wildly.

"It's okay. I'm not going to hurt you," he whispered against her ear. "I came to save you and Leah."

His words finally registered, and she stopped fighting, twisting to look up at him.

"I promise, Ruby. I'll get you and Leah out of here. Now I'm going to move my hand but don't scream. We have to be quiet. I don't want the man who kidnapped you to know I'm here, okay?"

She nodded and he moved his hand. She searched his face as he looked in her eyes. Snowflakes glittered in her strawberry-blond hair, and her eyes were huge with fear.

She was tough though, he could tell by her stubborn chin and the fight in her. And she looked so much like Leah that he fell in love with her instantly. "Are you all right, Ruby? Did he hurt you?"

"No," she cried. "But he's got Leah, and he has a gun, and he's going to kill her."

"No, he's not," Gage said soothingly. "I won't let him. Now listen to me. There's a police car down the drive, just a few feet. I want you to run to it, crawl inside and lock the doors. Can you do that?"

She nodded.

"Go. I'll bring Leah to you."

"'Kay." He gave her a gentle push, and she ran through the fog of snow as fast as her legs could carry her, her hair swirling around her in the wind.

Another gunshot sounded, and his blood ran cold. He had to get to Leah.

He crept toward the building, but saw Harry dragging Leah outside, a pistol in one hand. She was limp in his arms, and Gage's heart pounded.

Where was Charlie?

Wiggins headed to the spot where posts designated the new greenhouse was to be built. Gage glanced inside the building and saw Charlie lying on the floor near the door, blood pooling, his hand over his chest.

Gage stepped inside, knelt and checked for a pulse.

"Driscill?"

"It's just my shoulder. I'll live," he mumbled.

Gage nodded and moved back outside, then inched around the corner of the building. Wiggins had dumped Leah onto the ground, and was digging a hole with a shovel.

The son of a bitch.

Circling to the opposite side of the building, he crept slowly and silently up behind Wiggins, focusing on one thing and one thing only.

Saving Leah.

Wiggins was deep in his task, digging and slinging dirt to the side, creating a burial plot.

One he would never put Leah in.

Raising his gun, Gage forced himself not to look at Leah, to focus on Wiggins. Gage was an excellent shot, but it was dark and the blizzard conditions made it hard to see.

He spotted Wiggins's gun on the ground beside him. Gage crept closer, the sound of the shovel against dirt ominous in the silence. Wiggins wheezed a labored breath, rubbing at his forehead with his sleeve, and Gage closed the distance, raising the gun to the back of his head.

"Drop it, Wiggins. It's over."

Wiggins froze, then suddenly spun around and swung the shovel at Gage's knees.

Gage dodged the blow and fired, hitting Wiggins in the chest. He went down with a yelp, his eyes widening as he went into shock. Blood gushed from his chest, and Wiggins coughed and choked, struggling for a breath. He rasped loudly, his body jerked and then he went totally still as his last breath left him.

Gage grabbed the shovel and threw it into the woods, then ran to Leah, knelt and felt for a pulse. She was breathing, but Wiggins had knocked her out.

His heart hammering, he patted her face gently. "Leah, wake up. Can you hear me?"

Her chest rose and fell, and he patted her again. "Please, Leah, wake up, Ruby's waiting on you. She's safe and needs you."

Slowly she opened her eyes, blinking as if he was blurry. "Ruby?" she croaked.

"Ruby's fine. She's waiting in the police cruiser."

She gripped his arm to sit up. Her face twisted as she spotted Harry on the ground.

"He's dead," Gage said. "He can't hurt you or Ruby ever again."

"Thank God."

She swayed as they stood, and he lifted her in his arms and carried her around the side of the building. "I'm taking you to Ruby, then we need to call for an ambulance. Wiggins shot Charlie."

"I know." Her teeth chattered. "Is he…dead?"

"No, a shoulder wound."

"Good," she said as she leaned into his arms. "He saved me, Gage. He took the bullet that was meant for me."

So Driscill had tried to redeem himself.

Still, Gage would never forgive him or the others for what they'd done to Leah. Especially Jerry—he'd hate Jerry forever.

LEAH CRADLED RUBY close to her, hugging her inside the blanket Gage had given them, reassuring her that she was fine and that the man would never hurt them again.

Gage brushed a hand against Leah's cheek. "I'm going to let Charlie know that an ambulance is on the way."

Leah caught his hand and squeezed it. "Thank you, Gage."

He nodded, then went to Charlie while they waited on the ambulance.

"When we get home, we're going to get you a nice bath," Leah said softly to Ruby. "Then I'll wash your hair and comb it out, and you can put on your Christmas PJs and crawl into your bed with the unicorn comforter."

Ruby snuggled closer. "I lost Matilda," she said. "The mean man took her."

Leah shuddered, thinking of Harry's cruelty. "I know, honey, but we'll get you another one. Pippi is waiting for you."

"I love Pippi," Ruby said. "Leah?"

"Yeah, honey?"

"You think Santa will bring me the kitty?"

"I have a feeling he might."

"What should we name him?"

Leah laughed. "I don't know. Maybe we can make a list tomorrow before the Christmas musical. Your costume is all ready."

"Do the angel wings sparkle?"

"Yes, they do." She titled Ruby's face up to her. "You're going to be a beautiful angel, and I'm going to take a hundred pictures."

"And we'll sing 'Silent Night' with the lit candles?"

"You bet we will."

"Leah?"

"Yes?"

"Will Mr. Gage come with us?"

Leah bit her lip. "I don't know. We can ask him. Would you like that?"

She nodded and Leah hugged her tighter.

"Can I call you Mommy?" Ruby asked.

Tears blurred Leah's eyes. "I'd like that." She brushed her hair back. "In fact, that can be your Christmas present to me, honey."

GAGE SAT WITH Charlie until he heard the ambulance, then met the medics and escorted them to Charlie. Deputy Rainwater arrived a minute later, and Gage explained how he and Charlie had caught Harry.

"I'll wait here until the coroner comes for Wiggins's body," Rainwater said.

"Then I'll drive Leah and her daughter home," Gage said.

"They don't need medical care?"

"They seem to be okay." Ruby would need counseling, but Gage was certain Leah would see that she received it.

The snow was falling more heavily, collecting on the trees and ground as he strode back to the police car. Inside, Leah was holding Ruby, the two of them cuddled in the backseat. His chest swelled as he took in the mother-daughter picture.

He loved Leah.

But how did she feel about him?

She was grateful for his help and would have let him make love to her.

But now that Ruby was coming home and the danger was over, would she still want him? Or was he part of the past that she was desperate to put behind her?

Chapter Nineteen

Gage carried a sleepy-eyed Ruby up the steps. The firemen and CSI had left, but the scent of smoke still lingered, a reminder of the earlier attack on Leah.

And the fact that they'd almost made love.

"Are you sure you want to stay here tonight?" he asked.

She nodded. "This is our home, and Ruby needs to sleep in her own bed."

"I asked the crime unit to bring your gifts and Ruby's things back inside. But your room is a mess."

"I'll sleep with Ruby, and clean the room tomorrow," Leah said. "I don't want to leave her tonight."

He nodded, understanding that she'd want to be close to Ruby. But he didn't want to leave.

Only this wasn't his home. It was Leah and Ruby's.

And what if Ruby was Jerry's child?

Ruby snuggled against him, and his chest tightened. She was so little and innocent, yet she'd endured the last few days like a trouper—just like her mother. He could easily love the child just as he did Leah.

"Just put her here on the couch," Leah said. "I promised I'd wash her hair before bed."

He gently placed Ruby on the sofa and she stirred from sleep, fear lining her face. "Leah?"

Leah went to her. "It's okay, I'm here, honey."

Gage frowned, hating the ordeal Ruby had been through and wanting to stay and take care of both Leah and her daughter.

But he didn't belong.

"Okay, call me if you need me."

She nodded, then walked him to the door. "Gage, I don't know how to repay you for what you did."

He lifted his hand and stroked her hair, aching to hold her. "You don't have to repay me, Leah. It was my job." Although it had become so much more.

A strange look darkened her eyes. Ruby moved up behind her, and tugged her hand.

"Mr. Gage?" Ruby said.

Gage's heart melted. "What, Ruby?"

"You wanna come see me at our play tomorrow night? I'm an angel."

She sure was. He looked at Leah, desperate to know if she wanted him there. But her face gave nothing away.

"If you're too busy, it's all right," Leah said.

Disappointment washed over him. "I'll see," he said quietly.

Ruby yawned, and he said good-night, stepping outside into the blustery night. It was going to be a white Christmas, and Leah and her daughter would spend it together.

But dammit, he wanted to be a part of it.

Uncertainty nagged at him. If he couldn't, he didn't know if he could stay here.

Being in Sanctuary and not being with her would kill him.

LEAH STRUGGLED not to feel bereft when Gage left, but his comment about finding Ruby being his job stung. She'd thought it had become personal, that he cared about her, and when he'd held Ruby, she'd thought she'd seen affection in his eyes.

But the truth about the past created a chasm between them.

He'd said he didn't blame her, but still, she would be a reminder of his awful relationship with his adopted brother.

"Mommy?"

Leah's heart swelled at the sound of that word. "Yes, honey. Let's go get that bath."

She helped Ruby to the bathroom and ran some water, pouring bubblebath in. She wanted to know everything the man had said and done to her, and she'd make sure Ruby saw a counselor, but that could wait.

Ruby looked tired. Leah intended to give her every ounce of love she possessed and atone for every moment she'd lost with her little girl.

She scrubbed Ruby's hair and wrapped her in a big fuzzy robe. Ruby dashed into her room and slipped on her pajamas. They sat on the bed and Leah dried and brushed Ruby's hair, singing to her.

"I missed you," Ruby said. "I don't want to ever leave home again."

Leah pulled her into her arms and smiled. One day Ruby would grow up and be eager to leave, and she'd have to encourage her to go out on her own. But for now, she'd savor every moment she could with her little girl.

Finally Ruby crawled under the covers, and Leah lay down beside her. Ruby fell into a deep sleep and Leah closed her eyes, thanking God that she had Ruby back.

But an emptiness also settled in her chest. She missed Gage and wanted him to be a part of their lives.

Could they be a family, or was that impossible?

THE NEXT MORNING, Leah rose early, knowing she had a million things to do. First she arranged the presents under the tree, then tackled her bedroom, cleaning up the mess from the fire. She threw away the charred curtains and the rug, then scrubbed the room to alleviate the scent of smoke. Her bedding had to be trashed since the fabric had absorbed the smoky odor. It was such a mess she considered selling the house and moving, but it was the only home Ruby had ever known.

Maybe she'd paint the room after the holiday and re-decorate, making it more appealing.

Make it a room a man might want to stay in, as well.

Hope struggled to the surface. She'd been afraid half her adult life, running from relationships and people. But she was through running.

So why wasn't she going after Gage?

She loved him. And she wanted him in her life. But did he want her?

There was only one way to find out. She would no longer play the part of victim, the girl who kept quiet. If she wanted something, she'd go after it.

And she wanted Gage.

Ruby finally stirred and they ate cereal, cuddling on the couch and making a list of names for the kitten Santa was supposed to bring. Neighbors dropped by with food to welcome Ruby home.

As they worked side by side in the kitchen making a gingerbread house, Ruby looked up at her with icing on her chin. "Leah? I mean, Mommy?"

She smiled, knowing it would take them both some time to get used to the change. "What, honey?"

Ruby pursed her lips in thought, her freckles dancing on her nose. "Can Mr. Gage be my daddy?"

Leah almost laughed. Kids were so resilient. "I don't know. Mr. Gage and I, we have to see how things work out. Now let's get ready for the musical."

Ruby's eyes widened in excitement. "Then it'll be Christmas and Santa will come."

Ruby raced toward her bedroom, and Leah picked up

the phone to call Gage. Maybe he'd do her a favor and pick up the kitten. And when he brought it in the morning, maybe he'd stay for a while.

Maybe forever.

GAGE PAID A VISIT to Jerry's first thing in the morning. He intended to make sure Jerry never bothered Leah again. But he found Jerry packing.

Pleased that Jerry was leaving, Gage spent the morning scoping out facilities for GAI, in case he ended up staying. He found a huge Victorian house in the heart of Sanctuary down the street from Magnolia Manor with plenty of rooms that could be converted into office space for the team he planned to hire. His goal was to have the agency staffed and running full swing in the next year.

He vacillated over signing a lease, but promised the real estate agent that he'd let her know within the week.

Deputy Rainwater had phoned to say he'd like to work for him and Gage was happy to take him on. He also phoned Colby Watson, the federal agent who'd been to Sanctuary, and asked him to be on the lookout for Carmel Foster's runaway daughter.

His cell phone rang. Leah's number. His heart stalled, fear assaulting him. He quickly connected the call. "Leah, is everything all right?"

"Yes," she said softly. "But I wanted to ask you a favor."

"What?" Anything.

God, he had it bad.

"Would you pick up the kitten for me and bring it over in the morning?"

He gritted his teeth. That wasn't exactly an invitation into her life. "Sure. Just give me the address."

He scribbled it down and promised to arrive around dawn in case Ruby woke early.

Gage picked up the kitten, a little orange fur bundle with huge ears that licked him incessantly and curled up in a box and slept on the ride back to the cabin. He left it water and food, trying not to imagine Ruby's squeal of delight when she saw it.

Then he drove through town toward the small country church, passing the jewelry store.

His tires screeched as he turned into the parking lot before he even realized what he'd done.

He wanted to get Leah a gift, but what?

He knew what he *wanted* to give her, but would she accept it?

A half hour later, he entered the chapel, uncomfortable as he hadn't been in church in years. The small room over-flowed with people, close-knit neighbors who cared for one another, who'd all turned out to search for Ruby.

The kids filed in wearing costumes, and applause rang out. He spotted Leah up front, sitting next to Warren and his mother. It appeared they'd become friends despite everything.

Then the lights dimmed and the program began. Gage stood in the back, feeling oddly left out. When he'd been sent to the orphanage, he'd ached for a family. And he'd thought he'd found one with the McDermonts, but now they were gone.

Ruby stepped up in the angel costume, waving her sparkling wings, and he smiled.

He wanted a family. And he wanted that family to be with Leah and Ruby. He didn't give a damn who Ruby's birth father was.

The children began to sing "Silent Night" and everyone lit the candles and held them up, the glowing, flickering lights a reminder that it was Christmas, that miracles could come true.

Maybe he'd get lucky and have his own miracle.

Chapter Twenty

Leah woke at dawn, excited and nervous. She'd looked for Gage at the musical and spotted him in the back, but he'd left without speaking to them. She hoped he would agree to spend Christmas day with her and Ruby.

She baked cinnamon rolls, slid the turkey into the oven and turned on the Christmas tree lights. Content with the Christmas atmosphere, she paused to study the picture of the three of them—Leah, Ruby and her mother—last Christmas, and sadness welled in her chest.

"You were a great mother, Mom. I'm going to try to be like you, to be there for Ruby."

A soft knock jarred her from her melancholy, and she hurried to the door to let Gage in. He was holding a box with the tiny kitten in it.

"Oh, she's adorable," Leah whispered.

Gage grinned, and she took the box and set it underneath the tree. He went back to the car and returned with a bundle of presents.

"For Ruby and the kitten," he said.

"You didn't have to do that, Gage."

"I wanted to. It's just some chew toys and a climbing post."

"Thanks."

His dark eyes raked over her, stirring her hunger. "Did you sleep better last night?"

"It was heaven having Ruby home." He looked at the door as if he might leave, and she felt panic—she wanted to kiss him and beg him to stay. "Would you like coffee?"

He nodded and she poured them both a cup, then they moved by the fireplace. Ruby shuffled in, wearing red and white PJs, sleepy-eyed. But she soon spotted the tree and the kitten, and squealed in delight.

"Santa came! He brought my kitty!" She raced over and scooped up the wiggling orange furball, laughing as it licked her nose and cheek. "I'm gonna call you Kit Kat," she said with a giggle.

"I like that," Leah said.

Ruby placed the kitty on the floor, clapping and jumping up and down as it waddled around. She chased it and cuddled it against her again, her exuberant excitement ringing in the air.

Leah's heart swelled with love and happiness. Then she looked up at Gage and joy spread through her as warm affection shone in his eyes for her daughter.

She placed her hand on his cheek. "I love you, Gage."

His eyes darkened as he looked down at her. "God, Leah—"

"I know I ripped your family apart," she said softly, "and that it's complicated with Ruby—"

He shook his head. "No, it's not complicated at all. I love you, too, Leah."

Tears of joy pooled in her eyes. "You do?"

"I always have," he said in a low murmur. "But I was afraid I'd just be a reminder of Jerry," he said in a gruff voice.

"You're nothing like him." She stood on tiptoe and kissed him gently. "You're everything I've ever wanted in a man."

He removed a small present from his pocket. "I have a present for you, too."

Her eyes widened, her heart fluttering. "Gage?"

"Open it."

Her fingers trembled as he pushed it into her hands, and she tore open the paper. Inside, she found a jewelry box. Her heart sputtered as she opened the velvety case.

A solitary diamond in a platinum setting glittered in the box. "Oh, Gage."

He dropped to his knee by the Christmas tree, the lights shining in his eyes as he took her hand in his. "Will you marry me, Leah? Will you let me be your husband and a father to Ruby?"

Ruby ran over, hugging the kitten to her, staring at both of them wide-eyed.

"Mommy?"

Leah smiled and glanced at her daughter. "What do you think, Ruby? Should we marry Gage?"

"Yes," Ruby said with a squeal. "This is the best Christmas ever! Santa brought Kit Kat, and now I'm getting a daddy!"

Gage laughed with Leah, then pulled her into his arms and kissed her.

Beside them Ruby sang out, "Mommy and Daddy, sittin' in a tree, k-i-s-s-i-n-g. First comes love, then comes marriage, then comes Mommy with a baby carriage!"

Ruby slid between them, and they hugged her, welcoming her into their new family. Maybe next year for Christmas Ruby would get a little sister or brother.

AS GAGE EASED Leah down on the four-poster antique bed, his palms began to sweat. He wanted this night to be special, romantic, and he wanted to make love to his wife in this honeymoon suite with a perfect view of the mountain.

But he'd promised Leah he'd never push her. He could wait.

He didn't want to, but dammit, he loved her and he would do anything to make her happy. Including just holding her if that was what she needed him to do.

"You look amazing," he said, his heart hammering as he gazed into her eyes. "I always thought you were beautiful, Leah, but today you're radiant."

She stood and laced her hands around his neck. "That's

because I'm happy and in love." She brushed her lips across his, teasing him and making him instantly go hard.

He gestured toward a basket of goodies on the table. "Do you want some chocolate or fruit, or a bath?"

"Maybe some champagne," she whispered.

He arched a brow. "I thought you didn't drink."

"I don't," she said with a laugh. "But we should toast our marriage." She traced a finger along his jaw. "Besides, I'm not afraid of losing control with you." She kissed him gently. "I might even want to lose control."

He chuckled. "Well, I do believe my wife has a flirty side."

"Only for her husband."

"I like it. And I like the sound of that word." He kissed her, then popped the cork and poured them both a glass of champagne. "To my beautiful wife," he said. "I can't believe I'm lucky enough to have you."

Her eyes flickered with emotions. "I wanted you eight years ago, Gage." She sipped the champagne. "And I want you even more now."

He placed his glass on the table and reached for her. She came to him, her chest rising as she licked her lips. He lowered his head and claimed her mouth with his. She opened to him, and he tasted the champagne and the sweetness of her mouth, deepening the kiss until they were both breathing hard.

"I love you, Leah. But if you want me to stop at any time, all you have to do is say the word."

"I don't want you to stop," she said softly. "I want you to make love to me."

His pulse accelerated, hunger and a fierce need for her spiraling through him.

He threaded his hands through her hair, cupping the back of her neck and nibbling at the slender column, inhaling the fragrance of her skin, the sultry taste of her need. His hands glided over her shoulders and down to her waist. Then he cupped one breast in his hand, kneading the heavy weight. She moaned and moved against him, running her hands over his shoulders and arms, clinging to him as he stroked her thigh with his leg.

Slowly, he peeled off her ivory satin dress, gasping with pleasure at the sight of her breasts spilling over the lace bra and the skimpy see-through panties encasing her heat.

She freed him of his tie, flinging it on the velvet chair in the corner, a wicked gleam in her eyes. "I never knew undressing a man could be so much fun."

He threw his head back and laughed. "Sweetheart, have at it."

She licked her lips again, then did as he suggested, her gaze darkening with appreciation as she raked her eyes over his body. He took off her bra, his heart hammering as her breasts spilled into his hands and her nipples stiffened to peaks between his hungry fingers.

He loved her gently, kissing her and showing her with his tongue and hands how much he treasured her and the gift of her body. And when she kicked off her panties, and pulled him to the bed between her thighs, his sex ached to be inside her.

But he wanted her to know real pleasure—she would always come first.

He traced his tongue over one nipple, teasing, tasting, sucking the tip until she groaned and buried her hands in his hair. His fingers wandered over her flesh, stroking her, easing her legs apart, gently teasing her inner thighs and womanly folds. Then he lowered his head and licked a path down her belly.

She bucked and writhed, and he held her hips. She tasted like heaven, and he wanted her to know the intimacy of a lover's caress, of having a man give before receiving.

When she cried out with pleasure, he raised himself above her and looked into her eyes, wanting her to see how much he loved her as he slid inside her. Her eyes were full of passion, hunger, and she pulled him toward her, parting her legs to invite him inside.

Their gazes locked as he teased the tip of her warm opening with his sex, but he forced himself to move slowly, to gently glide inside her, inch by inch.

"Gage, please," she whispered.

He smiled, spurred on by her sultry plea, then buried his length deep inside her. She cried out again, clutching him as he pulled out and thrust inside her deeper. Moaning, she wrapped her legs around him, her body tightening as they built their rhythm, slowly at first, but becoming more frantic. And when she shuddered again, her body quaking with sensations, he joined her as his own release tore through him.

He kissed her again, their bodies connected as one, just as their lives and futures were.

He'd finally found the home he'd been searching for all his life. And it was with Leah.

And this time he'd stay forever.

* * * * *

Here is a sneak preview of
A STONE CREEK CHRISTMAS,
the latest in Linda Lael Miller's acclaimed
McKETTRICK *series.*

A lonely horse brought vet Olivia O'Ballivan to
Tanner Quinn's farm, but it's the rancher's love that
might cause her to stay.

A STONE CREEK CHRISTMAS
Available December 2008
from Silhouette Special Edition.

Tanner heard the rig roll in around sunset. Smiling, he wandered to the window. Watched as Olivia O'Ballivan climbed out of her Suburban, flung one defiant glance toward the house and started for the barn, the golden retriever trotting along behind her.

Taking his coat and hat down from the peg next to the back door, he put them on and went outside. He was used to being alone, even liked it, but keeping company with Doc O'Ballivan, bristly though she sometimes was, would provide a welcome diversion.

He gave her time to reach the horse Butterpie's stall, then walked into the barn.

The golden retriever came to greet him, all wagging tail and melting brown eyes, and he bent to stroke her soft, sturdy back. "Hey, there, dog," he said.

Sure enough, Olivia was in the stall, brushing Butterpie down and talking to her in a soft, soothing voice that touched something private inside Tanner and made him want to turn on one heel and beat it back to the house.

He'd be damned if he'd do it, though.

This was *his* ranch, *his* barn. Well-intentioned as she was, *Olivia* was the trespasser here, not him.

"She's still very upset," Olivia told him, without turning to look at him or slowing down with the brush.

Shiloh, always an easy horse to get along with, stood contentedly in his own stall, munching away on the feed Tanner had given him earlier. Butterpie, he noted, hadn't touched her supper as far as he could tell.

"Do you know anything at all about horses, Mr. Quinn?" Olivia asked.

He leaned against the stall door, the way he had the day before, and grinned. He'd practically been raised on horseback; he and Tessa had grown up on their grandmother's farm in the Texas hill country, after their folks divorced and went their separate ways, both of them too busy to bother with a couple of kids. "A few things," he said. "And I mean to call you Olivia, so you might as well return the favor and address me by my first name."

He watched as she took that in, dealt with it, decided on an approach. He'd have to wait and see what that turned out to be, but he didn't mind. It was a pleasure just watching Olivia O'Ballivan grooming a horse.

"All right, *Tanner,*" she said. "This barn is a disgrace. When are you going to have the roof fixed? If it snows again, the hay will get wet and probably mold…"

He chuckled, shifted a little. He'd have a crew out there the following Monday morning to replace the roof and shore up the walls—he'd made the arrangements over a week before—but he felt no particular compunction to explain that. He was enjoying her ire too much; it made her color rise and her hair fly when she turned her head, and the faster breathing made her perfect breasts go up and down in an enticing rhythm. "What makes you so sure I'm a greenhorn?" he asked mildly, still leaning on the gate.

At last she looked straight at him, but she didn't move from Butterpie's side. "Your hat, your boots—that fancy red truck you drive. I'll bet it's customized."

Tanner grinned. Adjusted his hat. "Are you telling me real cowboys don't drive red trucks?"

"There are lots of trucks around here," she said. "Some of them are red, and some of them are new. And *all* of them are splattered with mud or manure or both."

"Maybe I ought to put in a car wash, then," he teased.

"Sounds like there's a market for one. Might be a good investment."

She softened, though not significantly, and spared him a cautious half smile, full of questions she probably wouldn't ask. "There's a good car wash in Indian Rock," she informed him. "People go there. It's only forty miles."

"Oh," he said with just a hint of mockery. "*Only* forty miles. Well, then. Guess I'd better dirty up my truck if I want to be taken seriously in these here parts. Scuff up my boots a bit, too, and maybe stomp on my hat a couple of times."

Her cheeks went a fetching shade of pink. "You are twisting what I said," she told him, brushing Butterpie again, her touch gentle but sure. "I meant…"

Tanner envied that little horse. Wished he had a furry hide, so he'd need brushing, too.

"You *meant* that I'm not a real cowboy," he said. "And you could be right. I've spent a lot of time on construction sites over the last few years, or in meetings where a hat and boots wouldn't be appropriate. Instead of digging out my old gear, once I decided to take this job, I just bought new."

"I bet you don't even *have* any old gear," she challenged, but she was smiling, albeit cautiously, as though she might withdraw into a disapproving frown at any second.

He took off his hat, extended it to her. "Here," he teased. "Rub that around in the muck until it suits you."